"You've had some absolute whoppers of ideas in your time, but this one definitely gets the award."

He folded his arms across his broad chest and waited.

"I mean, you and me—a couple? Who's gonna believe that?"

He sighed. "Molly—"

"And to suggest that we'd ever be able to fool anyone—I mean, there are days we have difficulty just getting on well enough to still like each other as friends!" She started pacing in front of him.

He sighed again. "If you'd just—"

"We'd have to be able to look at each other without sniggering every two minutes. And as for the kissing thing—" She stopped pacing long enough to waggle a finger at him. "You do realize if we were actually dating we'd be expected to kiss and—well, other stuff like that...."

There was a deadly silence as they stared at each other in shock. Ryan swallowed hard. "I know that—"

Trish Wylie resides in the lakeland border county of Fermanagh in the north of Ireland. She splits her not-long-enough days between five horses, three dogs, writing and her fiancé, in roughly that order. (Though writing only comes third because the first two can't feed themselves.) She started writing in primary school, about imaginary people who lived on an island sponge in the middle of the bathtub, and has wanted to write for Harlequin® since she read her first romance novel in her early teens. She first tried writing romance when she was about seventeen, but realized that it might be an idea to fall in love and have her heart broken a few times before she attempted writing about it.

Always a little in love with her heroes, Trish prefers that, as in real life, they have a sense of humor. She likes to believe that these men are just around the corner!

Harlequin® is thrilled to bring you Trish Wylie's first book for Harlequin Romance®. We're sure you'll enjoy her lyrical voice and warm, passionate characters. In *The Bridal Bet* you'll meet Molly O'Brien and Ryan Callaghan, two friends with a lot of past... and an unexpected future!

Watch out for a new duet from Trish Wylie toward the end of 2005, in Harlequin Romance®!

THE BRIDAL BET

Trish Wylie

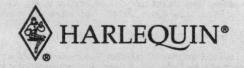

TORONTO • NEW YORK • LONDON
AMSTERDAM • PARIS • SYDNEY • HAMBURG
STOCKHOLM • ATHENS • TOKYO • MILAN • MADRID
PRAGUE • WARSAW • BUDAPEST • AUCKLAND

For all the old "Lisburn Crowd."
We turned out okay in the end, didn't we?

ISBN 0-373-03842-9

THE BRIDAL BET

First North American Publication 2005.

Copyright © 2003 by Trish Wylie.

www.eHarlequin.com

Printed in U.S.A.

CHAPTER ONE

'YES, I am still standing at the bottom of the ladder, and yes, I am looking straight up your dress.'

Ryan grinned and tried valiantly to avert his gaze. It wasn't easy. Molly O'Brien had great legs; he had never argued with that. In all his years as her nemesis, friend and elder brother figure he had never once been blind to her good points or her bad. The moment he glanced upwards he was awarded an eyeful of two of those good points....

'Callaghan, the moment I get down from here, you die.'

'Are you threatening to fall on me? 'Cos I should warn you, your wee body falling on me isn't likely to kill me outright. Now, if you were to be up a few feet more you might knock me out, but from where you are the best you're likely to do is bruise me a little.'

Molly laughed out loud, despite her best efforts not to. 'A good bruising would do you no harm, buster!'

'That's right, treat me rough, Moll. I can take it.' An obliging breeze lifted the edge of her dress and Ryan was forced to swallow hard as his eyes caught a glimpse of white lace. He felt an irritating warm flush cross his cheeks. 'Haven't you got that stupid creature yet?'

She stretched her fingers out an extra inch and was rewarded with the touch of soft fur. 'Good kitty, come to Mammy...ha!' She pulled him towards her chest. 'Gotcha. Next time you climb on the porch, Houdini, you can darn well get down on your own, and then I won't have to have that lump down there look where he shouldn't—you hear me?'

Ryan held the ladder patiently until she hit *terra firma.* Then he grinned a lop-sided grin at her. 'I could hear that, y'know.'

Molly tilted her head to look up at him. 'Mmm, you were supposed to. How anyone over six foot two can possibly have vertigo stuns me. If you were any sort of a gentleman you would have gone up there to rescue Houdini yourself instead of sending me up there!'

'I hate heights—you *know* I hate heights. And I still maintain if you didn't keep rescuing that stupid beast every time he gets stuck then he would soon learn how to get out of these messes on his own.'

She stuck her tongue out at him, then laughed. 'You always bring out my mature side. It's one of your less endearing qualities.'

Ryan bent down until his nose almost touched hers, his breath fanning her face. 'Molly, *all* my qualities are endearing. You just haven't noticed that yet.'

'You wish!'

After lifting the ladder down he stored it away beneath the porch, before following her inside the house they had been sharing for almost six months. As pretty much his best friend, Molly had been Ryan's sparring partner for as long as he had known her, and he had to admit it was fun spending time with her again. Almost like being kids again—well, almost.

Turning a pine stool around to sit astride at the breakfast bar, he watched as Molly moved around the kitchen. She was the same Molly he had known for nearly fifteen years, and yet since she'd come home from the States she was different somehow. Lately he'd found himself watching her, trying to see what it was.

With her back to him as she filled the kettle with water,

she felt the hair prickling on the back of her neck and smiled softly. 'You're staring again, Callaghan.'

'Who, me?'

'Yeah, you.'

'You know, you've really got to stop this ego trip. Thinking I have nothing better to do with my time than stand and stare at you.'

Turning the kettle on, she glanced at him from the corner of her eye. 'Sit and stare, you mean.'

She moved to lean her back against the counter top, folding her arms across her chest before awarding him one of her patented 'don't kid me' glares. 'And it's not the first time this week. What's up?'

Ryan plastered his best innocent look across his face and blinked at her with dark eyes. 'What do you mean, what's up? There's nothing up. Am I not allowed to look at you now?' Green eyes narrowed suspiciously as she watched his little act. 'You are such a bad liar, Callaghan. Come on, spill it....'

'Spill it? Ah now that would be one of those quaint American sayings of yours, would it? I make that about the twentieth one you've used this week.'

'Don't change the subject.'

'I'm not. I'm just saying, that's all. How long do you think it'll take to make you Irish again after spending six years going all Yank on us?'

Molly unfolded her arms and slowly moved across the room to face him over the breakfast bar. 'I have always been Irish and I will always be Irish, you great rat, and you know it!'

He leaned towards her. 'Now, Molly O'Brien, did you just go calling me a rat again?' His dark eyebrows raised in question as his eyes shone at her. 'Because you know that would be the third time today you've done that, and that would mean you owe me.'

Her eyes widened and then closed as she shook her head. He had been teasing her about her new accent and her Americanised ways ever since her return. He knew how riled she got at the taunts. 'I don't believe you. You tricked me into losing a bet and now you're going to gloat, aren't you?'

If her eyes had opened a second sooner she'd have seen him smile affectionately at her. As it was, he looked cool and calm when she looked into his eyes. 'What's the payment, rat face?'

'Ah now, I'll need to think about that for a while.' He stood up and replaced the stool before walking towards the doorway. 'There's no point in rushing these things—takes all the fun clean out of them. I'll tell you later at the dance.'

'We're gonna have to pre-set these, you know.'

He stopped at the door, grinning over his shoulder. 'Now, where would be the sense in that? I've got to keep you on your toes somehow.'

Molly lifted an available tea towel and threw it in his direction. 'Go away and do Park Ranger things before I'm forced to do something I'll regret, Callaghan.'

His deep laughter forced an answering grin from her. 'There you go, making promises you can't keep again. One of these days I think I might just stick around and see what that thing you might regret might be....'

'That'll be the day.'

Ryan lived to be outdoors. In all the time Molly had known him he'd been his happiest under an open sky. Being Head Park Ranger and running the daily operations of a large forest park was the ideal job for him and Molly knew it. She smiled at him across the crowd at the summer barbecue and dance held for the residents of the local village of Boyle, wondering how the villagers managed to take him seriously.

At that precise moment two businessmen and their wives—though it had to be said probably more so the wives—stood enthralled as he spoke. He was a well-respected member of the small community, and yet they never seemed to see the clownish side of him that Molly knew so well. She wondered how they'd react if they knew about the wicked sense of humour he possessed, and the rare talent he had for torturing his friends.

Taking a sip of warm red wine, she smiled up at the wide expanse of darkened blue sky. She breathed deeply. It was good to be home again. Nowhere else filled her soul with the same peace she felt in Ireland. Then she turned her attention to the crowd. It was a hobby of hers, people-watching.

The local community had grown considerably since she had been away, and there were more than a few faces she didn't know in the crowd. A sign of the times, she guessed, with a new bypass making it easier for people to commute to the larger towns for work. But the surroundings hadn't changed at all since the summers she had spent running wildly through the park's many acres and swimming in the often chilly waters of its lough.

As she turned to look across the dark waters a voice sounded close beside her.

'Hello, I don't believe we've met?'

Molly had long since ceased to believe in the tingling sensation described in romance novels when a woman heard a stranger's voice for the first time. But all of a sudden she understood it now. The man's voice was deep and undeniably sexy. Intriguing, even.

Turning, she found herself looking up at the brightest of

blue eyes. The handsome tanned face was one she didn't recognise.

She smiled, unconsciously brushing her auburn hair behind her ear. 'No, I think I'd probably have remembered meeting you.'

The fair-headed man smiled. 'That's exactly the reason I *knew* I hadn't met you.' He extended a large hand towards her. 'I'm Nick—Nick Scallon. I just moved into the house over by Doon Cottages.'

'Aha, that'd make you the property tycoon guy we've all heard so much gossip about for the last few months. You're running the holiday cottages now, then, I take it?' She shook his hand and was embarrassed to find he held onto her smaller hand for a moment longer than he needed to. 'You're the main topic of conversation in the supermarket, you know.'

'I'll just bet I am.' He looked down at her hand in his. Seeming to remember he needed to let go of it, he allowed it to slip from his hold. 'And you would be?'

Impressed was nearly her answer, but she managed to replace it with another. 'Molly O'Brien. I, uh, live over at Ryan Callaghan's.'

'Oh.'

She nearly fell over herself to correct his assumption. 'We're *friends*—I mean, I've known Ryan all my life—like a brother kind of a thing—I mean, we're not actually...'

Nick smiled as she blushed. 'Well, that's all right, then. He'll not kill me if I ask you to dance will he?'

Molly realised what an idiot she'd just made of herself and cringed inwardly. 'No, no. He'll not mind at all.'

Ryan was walking towards the refreshment table when they first caught his attention. He very nearly broke his neck with the speed of his own double-take. She hadn't even mentioned she'd met Nick Scallon, let alone knew him well enough to be drooling all over the man's shoes.

Selecting a bottle of beer from the table, he moved around the makeshift flooring until he found a tree to lean against.

God, could he hold onto her any tighter? How could she breathe? Ryan had seen Molly with other men before—well, maybe not that many *men*. It had been before she'd gone to the States, and she'd been younger then, so he supposed they had been—well, younger men. But he couldn't remember ever having been irritated by it. In a gut-wrenching, testosterone-induced kind of a way, anyway. What was with that?

After all she was Molly—just Molly. Molly, who he tortured on a regular basis, even though he should be mature enough to know better. It wasn't his business to be irritated by who she did or didn't dance with. It was just that...

He took a long swig of his beer before deciding that it was just that he'd got used to having her to himself again. At least since she'd come home. Yeah, that was it. If she started going out with Nick 'Mr Smarmy' Scallon then he wouldn't see as much of her, and he guessed he'd miss that. But then, he'd be seeing less of her when her house was finished and she moved out, so that was no big deal, right? Maybe it was just that massive sense of protectiveness he'd always felt towards her. That and the sudden dislike he had for Mr Smarmy. A *very* sudden dislike, in fact.

Nick said something that had Molly laughing and Ryan was slightly more irritated. He swigged down more amber liquid.

'Why, *Ryan*, what *are* you doing, hiding under here?'

He gulped more beer. *Hiding from limpet-like women?* This was just great—his night was completed now that

Maura Connell was by his side. With curiosity he wondered how someone so well spoken could manage to have the same effect on his nerves as fingernails down a blackboard. Somehow he managed to force a smile.

'Maura, how lovely to see you—and may I say how...' His eyes glanced down over the expensive trouser suit he thought completely over-the-top for an outdoor barbecue. 'How very, uh, smart you look.'

Her brown eyes narrowed slightly but she recovered quickly. 'Why, thank you. You men are just always so flattering with your words. Especially strong, outdoorsy types like yourself. But I guess we women are used to it by now.'

Thanks. 'That's very understanding of you.' He glanced across the dance floor. Were they dancing closer? How'd that happen? *Osmosis?*

Maura noticed his frown and followed the line of his gaze. She smiled silkily. 'Well, I see Molly has an eye for the money in town. I didn't realise she knew Nick.'

Nick. Ryan noted how Maura spoke his name as if she knew him intimately. 'They're just dancing. There's no reason to get jealous.'

'*I'm* not the jealous one here, Ryan.' She linked her arm through his, moving closer to his side. 'I think we both know where my interests lie, and at least with Molly dancing with Nick the rumour mill can have a rest about you two. And I can take more of a public interest in you myself. I think it's about time you and I got to know each other better.'

He coughed to clear her strong perfume from the back of his throat, gently removing her arm from his. 'What little rumour about us two would that be, Maura?'

It was notable how he had managed to evade her proposition. Maura wasn't best pleased by the snub. 'Why, half the village thinks you and Molly are sleeping together. Didn't you know?'

'*What?*'

'Oh, come on, Ryan. It's a small community, an old-fashioned one at that. What else did you think they were going to say about you two living together?' She smiled, seeming to forgive him for the recent snub. 'But we could put paid to that rumour simply enough, you know....'

He couldn't resist baiting the stupid woman. 'If it *was* a rumour we certainly could.'

Maura ran an elegantly manicured hand across her smooth blonde hair, watching Molly and Nick dancing. 'Well, if it's not a rumour then Nick will be all the more interested. From what I hear he's quite the ladies' man in Dublin, whether they're spoken for or not. But I'll understand if you want to pretend you *are* a couple to engage his interest in your little friend. He'd be quite a catch for her.'

She turned her attention back to Ryan. 'And once *she's* out of the way I'm sure you'll realise that *I'm* the most suitable choice for you, Ryan. No one else can advance your placing in this community like I can, and we both know it. We'd make the perfect couple.' She sighed dramatically. 'But I won't wait for ever.'

Ryan watched as she strode away and then raised his eyes heavenwards. 'I sincerely hope not.'

'You don't mind if I steal Molly, do you?' Ryan tried not to look too pleased as he interrupted the dance.

'Of course not, Ryan.'

Both men knew he lied, and they each knew that the other knew.

Ryan grinned. 'Thanks.'

Nick looked at the taller man with chilly eyes which

warmed noticeably as he looked back at Molly. 'I'll see you later, and maybe we'll go for that midnight swim.'

She giggled like a schoolgirl. Ryan was forced to look and see where *his* Molly had gone.

'I'll hold you to that, you know.'

Side by side they watched as Nick left the dance floor and was accosted by Maura.

'' *'I'll hold you to that you know.'* '' Ryan mimicked her in a high-pitched voice before laughing as he swung her into a dance. 'What was that supposed to be?'

'You can take a running jump off the nearest pier, Callaghan!'

He thumped one large fist against his broad chest. 'You wound me deeply, old pal of mine. You're not honestly going to tell me you like that man?'

'And why shouldn't I?' Green eyes blazed up into familiar dark ones. 'He's a charming, handsome, sophisticated, rich man. So naturally I'm going to find him completely gross!'

'Don't tell me—that'd be another of those quaint American sayings, wouldn't it?'

She thumped his shoulder before placing her hand there. 'You are such an absolute rat. I don't even know why I like you at all. Can you remind me?'

He leaned down towards her, his voice low and intimate. 'Because deep down you truly love me and you know it, that's why.'

Molly shook her head, but her eyes had softened and a smile was teasing the corners of her mouth. 'Well, if that's what you want to think, you just keep livin' the dream.'

They were silent for a moment as the music slowed and hung on the warm evening air. Ryan glanced up at the newly formed curtain of stars above them and sighed. 'Maura Connell says the man's a well-known womaniser.'

'She's the girl that would know, right enough.'

He smiled down at her. 'Meow. Seriously, though, wouldn't you rather know that, one way or another?'

Molly raised one eyebrow and looked him straight in the eye. '*Maybe* he's changed. Maybe he's moved to the country to get away from that reputation and meet someone genuine. Has that occurred to you inside that over-protective head of yours?'

If any thought occurred to him it was only the irritating one that recognised that Molly might genuinely have an interest in Mr Smarmy. Another thought swiftly followed. He, Ryan Callaghan, didn't like that idea one little bit. But then, that was only because—as Molly rightly pointed out—he was her protector. It was his job. Yeah, that was it.

'There's one way to find out for sure.'

Green eyes narrowed. 'Oh, yeah, and what might that be?'

'Maura reckons he'll be all the more interested in you if he thinks you're involved with someone else.' He couldn't look her in the eye. 'And apparently half the town *already* thinks you're involved with someone else, so that could be why he approached you in the first place.'

Molly noticed that he couldn't meet her gaze, and she knew she wasn't going to like where the conversation was headed. '*Who* do they think I'm involved with?'

Ryan cleared his throat and found his eyes focused on her mouth for some unknown reason. 'Me.'

She burst out laughing. 'You're kidding? That's utterly ridiculous. You and me? As if!'

'Well, that's what comes of sharing a house with one of the town's most eligible men.' He raised his chin indignantly, his dark eyes sparking with barely hidden irritation.

'Not everyone looks at me and sees some elder brother figure, all safe and reliable.'

'Safe and reliable—oh, yeah, that's how I see you right enough.' She was still laughing.

Ryan's anger rose. 'Well, maybe if you just took the time to notice you'd see that I'm actually not that damn bad!'

Her eyes widened at the hard edge to his voice. He was, what, angry that she thought the idea of her being attracted to him was ridiculous? No, that just couldn't be. No way. Not her Ryan. Not her 'safe and reliable' Ryan. She blinked at him.

He glared down at her.

Molly smiled, attempting to ease the sudden tension between them. 'Poor baby.'

Ryan's eyes softened the smallest amount, so small an amount that someone who didn't know him as well as Molly did would never have noticed it. But notice it she did, and almost sighed with relief. 'Look, Callaghan, Nick Scallon seems like a perfectly nice guy. I don't see what you have against him.'

'I have plenty against him if he's chasing after you for some short-lived affair.'

Molly frowned up at him. 'You don't know that!'

'How do you know he's not?'

She shook her head. 'You're being really stupid about this.'

Ryan smiled sarcastically. 'You wanna bet?'

'Ryan, quit it.'

'No. C'mon Molly.' He squeezed his arm tighter against her waist, drawing her body closer to his. 'If you're so convinced that he's such a nice guy then you should stand by your convictions.'

She allowed her body to move in time with the music,

matching the gentle sway of his hips. 'And how exactly do I do that, then?'

Ryan's smile was slow, and a challenge was lighting up in the back of his eyes. 'By proving me wrong. Go out with me, pretend we're an item for a few months, and we'll see just how nice a guy Mr Nick Scallon is. If he continues chasing you then you'll know exactly what his intentions are.'

The air was forced out of her lungs. 'You're off your trolley!' She glared at Ryan in amazement as he pulled her off the dance floor towards the walkway at the loughside.

He knew the warning signs of an impending O'Brien explosion and decided the further away she was from the general population, the less the fallout would be. 'It's not like you to go chicken on me, O'Brien.'

'Chicken?'

'Yeah, chicken.' He stopped and stared down at her. 'If you don't think you can handle the fact that I'm right, *as usual*, then say so.'

Snatching her arm away from him, she marched to the darker end of the walkway. Once there she turned to face him so quickly that he almost crashed into her. 'You've had some absolute whoppers of ideas in your time, but this one definitely gets the award.'

He folded his arms across his broad chest and waited.

'I mean, you and me—a couple? Who's gonna believe that?'

He sighed. 'Molly—'

'And to suggest that we'd ever be able to fool anyone—I mean, there are days we have difficulty just getting on well enough to still like each other as friends!' She started pacing in front of him.

He sighed again. 'If you'd just—'

'We'd have to be able to look at each other without

sniggering every two minutes. And as for the kissing thing—' She stopped pacing long enough to waggle a finger at him. 'You do realise if we were actually dating we'd be expected to kiss and—well, other stuff like that....'

There was a deadly silence as they stared at each other in shock. Ryan swallowed hard. 'I know that—'

She recommenced the pacing. 'It's the most ridiculous suggestion you've ever made, Callaghan, and you should know that, for crying out loud!'

'O'Brien—'

She stopped again and looked up into his eyes. 'I mean, honestly, what makes you think for one second we could fool anyone?'

Ryan frowned at her. 'Methinks the girl protests too much.'

'And just what does that mean?'

'Maybe you're too frightened to kiss me.'

Her eyes widened, fire glinting in their depths. 'Me? Frightened, of you? What in hell is there for me to be frightened of?'

He stepped closer, his body almost touching hers. Towering over her smaller frame until any dim light was almost obscured, he leaned down towards her. 'Maybe you might just *like* kissing me.'

'You wanna bet?'

'Well, actually, yes, I do.' His gaze was steady. 'I thought we'd established that fact.'

Her mouth gaped. 'I don't believe this. As if I'd *like* kissing you, of all people! Like as in *enjoy*? Like as in, *participate*—'

He did the only reasonable thing he could think of to shut her up. He hauled her body to his and kissed her.

At first Molly couldn't believe what he was doing. This was Ryan Callaghan. The Ryan she had known for half her life. The Ryan who, along with her soulmate Kieran, had managed to alternately torture, humour and protect her most of the way through her late teens. They'd been the three musketeers back then—almost invincible. She had thought she knew Ryan better than anyone else on the planet. It should have felt like kissing a brother. Somehow it didn't.

It felt—well, it felt nowhere near as awful as it could have been. In fact, it wasn't altogether unpleasant. In fact...

This just couldn't be right.

Ryan couldn't believe he was doing what he was doing. He was actually kissing Molly! Hello—earth calling Ryan. What *was* he doing? Then he forgot for a moment as he felt her mouth soften against his. Good Lord, he was kissing Molly. And, hell, but it felt good. Too good. He moved his mouth over hers, felt her small sigh against his lips. She was so warm, and sweet-tasting, and soft, and—

'Oops, sorry Mr Callaghan.' There was a childish giggle. 'We didn't see you there.'

They pulled away from each other, both staring at the two Collins children who had materialised by their side. Ryan found his voice first. Well, he assumed it was his voice. The sound certainly seemed to come out of his mouth, so it pretty much had to be his. 'That's okay, kids. Don't worry about it.'

The children looked backwards and forwards at the two adults, giggling again. The fair-haired girl waved at Molly before turning back into the darkness with her brother.

'See.' Her voice was the loudest of stage whispers. 'Mammy said they were goin' together. Let's go tell her she's right.'

Her brother's voice got louder as they moved further away. 'I'm telling her first!'

The echo of running footsteps bounced across the still water of the lough. 'No, you're not! I am!'

Ryan stared into the darkness as if he could still see them while Molly stared at his broad back. 'Callaghan—'

'Well, I guess that takes care of the kissing bit. They seemed fairly convinced.' He turned to look at her. 'Don't you think?'

'Oh, *you*—you'll just do *anything* to prove a point, won't you?' The burst of laughter sounded false, even to her own ears. For the first time in a very long time she felt awkward in his company. Unable to look him in the eye. 'But surely you can see this is a really dumb-ass idea?'

With only a moment's hesitation he reached down to frame her face with his large hands, forcing her to look at him. 'Protest noted. But, hey, come on, O'Brien.' He smiled a lop-sided smile at her, the one women always seemed to find endearing. 'It'll be hilarious. And we've already started the jungle telegraph talking. Since when have you ever chickened out of one of our bets?' He raised a dark eyebrow. 'Unless you're prepared to admit I'm right about Scallon.'

They stared at each other for a few seconds. Then, suddenly afraid that he might try to convince her some more, Molly moved back, out of his hold. She had never turned down one of Ryan's bets. Never allowed him the upper hand in their long relationship. And she wasn't about to start now.

She liked Nick Scallon, for crying out loud. He was the most attractive man she'd met in a good while. And she could think of nothing more rewarding than proving Ryan wrong about him. So if that meant she'd have to play charades for a few weeks then she could manage that. Really, she could. Piece of cake. And Ryan's forfeit would be hell...

Raising her chin to look at him, she smiled calmly. 'Okay, Callaghan, you're on. Let's just hope—' she moved close to him to brush an imaginary speck of dirt from his shirt '—you can take the heat.'

Ryan stared at her, his throat suddenly dry. What had he started? From past history he just knew that his payback would be a nightmare. Molly would make sure of that.

He grinned. *Bring it on.*

CHAPTER TWO

End of summer—fifteen years ago

'FRIENDS don't kiss.'

'Ever?'

Molly thought for a moment, her long legs tucked beneath her on the large sofa. It was the last night of the summer holidays and in the morning their two families would part again for another year. To celebrate the last evening they had had a huge barbecue by the lough before returning to Ryan's family's summerhouse. While the adults had drunk wine, chatting on the porch, the two kids had sat themselves in front of a video in the family room.

'Never.'

Ryan studied her profile carefully. 'What about when they say goodbye or wish each other a happy birthday?'

'That's different. Those are *friendly* kisses.'

'And the difference would be…?' She had piqued his interest and he wondered just what the extent of her knowledge could be at her age.

Molly avoided looking directly at him. Instead she kept her gaze focused on the television screen as she watched the source of their debate. They had been watching *When Harry met Sally*.

Out of the corner of his eye he had seen Molly blush a crimson-red during the café scene when Meg Ryan had demonstrated her talent for faking it. He had impressed himself by not laughing at her reaction. After all, it wasn't that he was that much more experienced than she was. A few fumblings in the darkness of a cinema or the back seat of a friend's car on a Saturday evening hardly made for a sex-life to brag about.

'You know.' She blushed again.

'Yes, I do know.' He smiled teasingly. 'I'm just curious to see if you do.'

Molly knew she should never have allowed this particular debate to begin. They didn't talk about stuff like this, and she was so embarrassed she wanted to have the sofa open up and swallow her.

'Well, let's just say I know the difference.'

'So, go on, then.'

'Fine.' By the time she spun to face him he'd already realised that he'd sparked her temper. It was her best defence in times of difficulty. And, boy, did she have a temper. 'You want to ruin our last night by being dumb and teasing me, then that's just fine. I don't really know, and you know I don't really know. I've never been kissed by a boy before. Not *that* way. Satisfied now? But I know there *should* be a difference.'

Ryan reached out and touched her arm. 'I wasn't trying to be mean. I was just wondering what you'd say.'

'Well, now you know.' She pulled her arm away from him and leaned back, her mouth pouting slightly. 'And how am I ever supposed to find out when I look like this? Boys don't kiss girls who look like me. They kiss pretty girls.'

'I thought you said boys were stupid?'

A frown creased her forehead. 'They are. But I guess it would be nice to have one even slightly interested in kissing me.'

Ryan smiled his lop-sided smile as she glanced at him from the corner of her eye. 'O'Brien, I'll make you a deal.'

Turning her head towards him, she raised an eyebrow. 'What kind of deal?'

'Well…' He leaned towards her, his voice low. 'If you haven't found out what it's like to be kissed by the time you're eighteen, *I'll* kiss you.'

Her eyes widened. *'You?'*

'Yes, me.'

Molly stared. 'Kiss *me*?'

'Yes.' He nodded. 'Kiss you. On your eighteenth birthday.'

She continued staring at him, as if suddenly seeing a side of him she'd never noticed before. Then she laughed and laughed, until tears fell from her eyes.

'Not in this lifetime.'

'I heard a rumour today in the newsagent's.'

Molly didn't lift her head as her friend and neighbour-to-be perched herself against the counter in front of her. Molly had opened the new gift shop in the forest park with Kate not long after coming home. She used one side of the store to display and sell mounted copies of her work, her one true love. Photography.

They had spent the morning selling various mugs, sticks of rock, key chains and guidebooks to two coachloads of tourists, as well as two of Molly's more expensive photographs of wildlife on the lough. So it was the first opportunity they'd had to talk since the weekend's barbecue.

Molly knew only too well what rumour Kate was referring to.

'Did you, now?'

'Uh-huh.'

'Well, they do say the newsagent's is the place to get news.' Still she didn't look up from the counter.

Kate waved her hand underneath Molly's nose until she looked at her. 'You know rightly what rumour I'm talking about, and don't you dare tell me you don't.'

'Come on, Kate, we both know how active kids' imaginations can be.' She tried her best to look sincere as she smiled at Kate, one of her closest friends. As she looked at Kate's trusting eyes she also remembered the crush she had had on Ryan when they were teenagers. But Kate was a married woman now, and happily heavy with child.

Her friend smiled smugly. 'I don't think I mentioned any kids.'

Molly blushed a fiery red, which she was sure wasn't matching her hair colour well. 'Kate, I'd really rather not talk about this.'

'Oh, no, you don't. I wouldn't miss this for the world.' She made herself comfortable leaning on the counter. 'Tell Auntie Kate all about it, and don't you dare skip any details.'

As she looked at her friend Molly knew she couldn't tell her the truth. Kate had never understood the challenges that she and Ryan had aimed at each other over the years. Kate was a happily—no, *blissfully* married woman, who adored her husband and wanted the rest of the world to be as in love as they were. How could Molly tell her why they were doing this? It would be easier to tell her the version of the truth that she wanted to hear, and then she and Ryan could just 'split up', as they'd planned, in three months' time. Kate would be none the wiser. Simple.

'What do you want to know?'

Kate hit her on the shoulder. 'Aw, come on, Molly. Did Ryan kiss you at the barbecue or not?'

That at least wasn't a lie. 'Yes, he did.' She blushed again.

'And?'

'And what?'

Kate sighed dramatically. 'It's like getting blood out of a stone. What was it like? Why did he kiss you now, after all this time? What's going on? 'Cos you *know* I've always wondered what it was with you two.'

Molly's eyes widened. She stared incredulously at her friend. 'You have? How come you've never said so? I mean, you of all people have always known how I felt about Ryan, so what on earth made you think—?'

'Molly, it's Ryan Callaghan we're talking about, here. I could never understand why you can't see what's absolutely plain as day to everyone else with a pulse. The man is *gorgeous*.'

'*Ryan* is? Are you nuts? I've called him many things in my time, but gorgeous was never one of them.' She laughed. 'He's just Ryan.'

Kate's eyebrows raised until they disappeared under her fringe. 'When was the last time you looked at him?' She grinned widely. 'Last Saturday night not included, of course.'

'That's not fair. I look at him.'

She felt Kate's eyes follow her as she moved away from the counter to rearrange the prints on the opposite wall, filling in the recent gaps that had appeared.

'Really? So you'll know what colour his eyes are, then.'

'That's stupid. I know that—they're dark.'

'Dark what?'

Molly's hands stilled as she thought, and then she smiled into thin air as she gained a mental image. 'Brown—you know—like that melted chocolate in the ad.'

'My goodness, Miss O'Brien, I had no idea you cared.'

Molly froze as Ryan's voice sounded close to her ear. She hadn't heard him enter the shop. She turned to look at him, finding his eyes glittering in a 'gotcha' kind of a way.

She stared as he turned to wink at Kate. 'Hi, Kate, how are ya?' Then, looking back into Molly's eyes, he added, 'Do go on. I could stand a few more compliments.'

'You rat. How long have you been in here?' She set her hands on his chest to push him out of her way. Instead he stood his ground, and placed his hands over hers to hold them against him. She could feel the beat of his heart against his shirt, was far too aware of his warmth, and was desperately tempted to kick him in the shins. 'Get out of my way!'

'Not 'til you agree to come swimming this evening. It's grand and warm outside. I thought we could eat over by the shore at Doon.'

She glared straight into his *melted chocolate* eyes, following their gaze as they swept back to Kate's grinning face. 'Don't you think she should come swimming, Kate, on a lovely night like this will be?'

Kate positively glowed back at him. 'Oh, definitely, Ryan.'

'See?' He looked back at her and immediately found himself looking at her mouth. A memory hit his mind uninvited and he frowned slightly. 'Kate agrees.'

Molly studied his frown, noticed where he was looking, and without thinking moistened her lips with the tip of her tongue. Dear Lord, but this little game was nearly too easy. 'Okay, you win. I'll go.'

Momentarily distracted by what she'd done with her tongue, Ryan had to take a second to focus on what she'd just said. 'Okay. Uh, I'll see you later, then.'

Molly smiled at his expression. 'Okay.'

'Right.'

Ryan looked at Molly, and Molly looked right back. Kate coughed and the world rocked back into place.

'Right, then.' Ryan grinned, released her hands and swung on his heel to leave the shop. 'Bye, ladies.'

Kate watched him leave and then turned to Molly, fanning her face with one hand. 'Is it just me, or did it just get real warm in here?'

Having spent the entire morning dodging questions from the ever curious Kate, Molly decided to escape the shop at lunchtime. She got sandwiches and a carton of juice from the cafeteria and then headed out into the warm June sunshine to sit by the main harbour.

Sunglasses on, she took a moment to soak in the atmosphere before tearing open the sandwiches and looking around. With hourly boat tours from the lough's main harbour, tourists were milling around in an assortment of holiday clothing. It didn't take long for her to pick Ryan out of the crowd, with him easily one of the tallest men there.

Gorgeous was never a word she would have associated with Ryan. Brad Pitt, yes. But Ryan Callaghan? Nope. Not that she thought he was troll-like. She frowned behind her sunglasses. So, what was he?

In her capacity as an experienced crowd-watcher she glanced around to see if she could find any good-looking men to compare him with. Purely for scientific purposes, of course. She found a fair-haired American who had flirted with her in the shop earlier and then looked at them both.

The American was quite tall—probably six feet—but slim, as was usually typical of taller men. Ryan, on the other hand, was broad across his shoulders and chest. Not *fat*. Quite definitely not fat. But broad.

The American's hair was fair, while Ryan's hair was a rich dark brown—so dark that when the light hit it it shone. Biting into her sandwich, Molly supposed that was fairly attractive.

The American had an open smiling face, with pale eyes that had teased when he'd flirted with Molly. Ryan's face could be lots of different things, depending on his mood at the time. But most of all, regardless of his straight, even features and strong chin, he had an honest face. Molly had always liked the fact that she could read just about every emotion from Ryan's face.

A soft smile touched her mouth as she watched him run across the harbour to give a small girl the stuffed bear she had just dropped. The little girl smiled, then giggled as he spoke to her, and Molly didn't have to see his face to know what it would be like. He'd always had that gentle look in his eyes when he'd teased her the first year they met. Without trying he had a way of drawing a smile out of a person, no matter how old they were.

That was the one thing she would never deny about Ryan. He was a genuinely nice guy. Molly smiled all the more when she thought about how much he would hate being told so, but he was.

Green eyes followed him until he walked out of her sight, his body moving in long strides that spoke of a silent confidence in his own strength. Then, her gaze falling onto the water, Molly finished her lunch.

Kate was right. She had never really thought about it, but Kate was right. Ryan *was* a gorgeous man. More than that, he was a nice, caring, gorgeous man. Shame, really. He just wasn't Molly's usual type. She'd never even been attracted to someone like him in her entire life. Just as well, she surmised, otherwise she might have got hurt in this latest game of theirs.

Molly's eighteenth birthday

It wasn't Ryan who kissed Molly on her eighteenth birthday. By then their worlds had changed and so, in many ways, had they. By her eighteenth birthday the two friends had become three, and then two of the three had become a pair. 'I can't believe you kept him secret from me for so long,' Molly challenged him with one elegantly raised eyebrow. 'Did you do it to torture me, or were you waiting 'til I had straight teeth?'

'As if I'd want to inflict you on any of my other friends.'

She surprised him then, by leaning forward and planting a warm kiss on his cheek. 'I love you, you know.'

Ryan wiggled his eyebrows ridiculously. 'Yeah, yeah— you and half the female population. I know.'

One elegant fingernail tapped on the end of his nose. 'Well, I was first, and don't you forget it.'

He reached out to steady her arms as she swayed towards him, smiling indulgently. 'And you, my red-haired friend, are a little the worse for birthday juice, aren't you?'

'Me? Why, Callaghan, I'm shocked you could even think such a thing.' She wrapped her arms around his waist, smiling up at him from his shoulder. 'But I am having a really great birthday. How 'bout you?'

Dark eyes shone down into green. 'It's not my birthday.'

'I know that. But are you having a great time?'

'With you? Always.' Molly frowned at him with an all too familiar pout on her full lips. 'You're teasing me.'

'Would I?'

'Yes. But you know what?'

'Go on, O'Brien, amaze me.' He smiled again. 'What?'

'I forgive you.'

Placing one strong arm around her slender waist, he half carried her towards an empty table. 'Well, I'm relieved about that. Now, why don't you just have a wee rest at this little table for a while and I'll find you some nice birthday coffee?'

Slumping down into the offered chair, Molly looked up at him. She frowned for a moment, looked around, and then patted the chair beside her. 'Sit down. I want to talk to you.'

'I'll just get some of that nice birthday coffee first.'

'No!' She grabbed hold of his shirtsleeve. 'No, *now*.'

Ryan watched as the wheels slowly turned in her head. Then she smiled at him. Looking at him from beneath long darkened eyelashes, she was positively flirtatious, and for some reason he couldn't stop himself from noticing it. Damn but she'd grown up. And it wasn't just the removal of her braces that had got her noticed by Kieran, his university roommate. She just seemed to have blossomed overnight.

Almost in slow motion, he sat down beside her. 'What's up?'

'Do you think I'm pretty?'

The question caught him off guard. Especially considering he'd already begun to notice how she looked. For a split second he looked like a rabbit caught in the headlights of a car.

Molly giggled musically. 'Why, Callaghan, I do believe for the first time ever I've managed to make you speechless. Happy Birthday me.'

He tried to stand up. 'I'll just get that coffee. I'd really like a cup, wouldn't you?'

She placed her hand on his thigh and pushed him back into the chair. Another dangerous smile. 'Don't avoid the subject at hand.'

Ryan was too busy trying to ignore 'the subject at hand'. The burning sensation on his thigh where her hand rested. Hadn't anyone told her what happened to twenty-one-year old males whenever good-looking females touched them that close to...?

He carefully removed the hand, placing it into the safety

of her own lap. 'Why would I avoid it? Of course you're pretty, Moll. That brace thing being off really helps.'

'Is it just the brace?' She leaned in close to him, her voice low. 'Is it just the brace, or have I changed at all—you know, *anywhere else*?'

If that rabbit didn't move soon it was going to get squooshed. A blink, then another, and then Ryan's brain started to work. 'Uh, what exactly are you fishing for?'

'Have you noticed anything *different* about me?' Her face was dangerously close to his. 'I mean, since you last saw me?'

Ryan swallowed hard to moisten his dry throat. Wow, but she smelled good—all soapy and slightly perfumey. Like flowers. *Hello, Ryan! Get a grip here. Hormone alert.*

'In what way, exactly?'

'You tell me.'

Molly stood up in front of him and turned full circle before holding her arms out at her sides. 'How do I look to you?'

Ryan did as he was bid and looked at her. He took a real good, long look at her. She was sensational. Really. He'd never thought of himself as a sexist kind of guy who ogled women's legs, but—wow. In a split second he decided he was a legs man. Not that he hadn't known that Molly had legs. Hell, he'd seen them in shorts or swimsuits every summer for the past four years. But not like this. Not encased in the sheerest of black stockings with her feet in the silliest strappy high heels he had ever seen. Not displayed to the world from beneath the teeniest of miniskirts. Had she actually paid money for that scrap of material?

'Well?'

'Huh?'

'Well? What do you see?'

He waved away her protests with one arm. 'I'm still looking.'

She had the smallest waist he thought he'd ever seen. Was she too skinny? Was that it? Did she have some kind of dumb obsession with her weight? No. His eyes travelled upwards. No, her weight was just fine. She had breasts now—small, full breasts that peeked out at him from the deep vee of her tight top. Maybe he was a breasts man after all. Then he looked back down at her legs. Nope. Still a legs man.

Then he looked up at her face. The freckles had faded down over the years. From somewhere she had got this creamy complexion. Full moist lips that drew into a wide smile over perfectly straight white teeth. *Thank you, Mr Orthodontist.* Wide green eyes above an elegantly upturned nose...

A hand waved in front of his face. 'Well—can you see it?'

His voice was sharp. 'Damn it, O'Brien, see what?' He'd seen plenty, and it irritated him that he'd noticed as much as he had. 'You look just fine to me.'

'*Fine?* I look just *fine?*' She looked annoyed. 'Well, thanks a bunch, big man.'

'Oh, hell.' Ryan ran long fingers through his short hair. 'What am I supposed to notice?'

With a sigh he could hear above the newly started music, she moved forwards. Placing one slender hand on either side of his face, her eyes smiled into his. 'Don't you see it, Ryan? I'm in *love.* For the first time in my life I'm in love. And it's with your friend. Thanks to you, I'm going to find out exactly what it's like to be with that someone who *really* matters.'

Ryan's gut twisted. How could he have known? How could he have seen that his two friends would end up this wrapped in each other? He'd met Kieran his first term at university in Dublin and had instantly liked the guy. With his golden good looks and extrovert nature he was popular on campus. And so much more outgoing than Ryan himself. He had an ease about him that people instantly took to.

Captain of the rugby team, top of his class in business studies, rich family in Galway. The guy had everything. All the criteria that overly protective brother figures would look for in a boyfriend for someone they really cared about. So why did he suddenly wish they'd never met?

Much as she hated to admit it, Ryan had been right. Yet again. This time about the evening being perfect for swimming at Doon Shore. Situated on the side of the lough furthest from the main tourist amenities, it tended to be a place that only the locals and a few cruise boat tourists ever knew about. Which also meant that on a sunny summer evening it was normally filled with townsfolk. Most of whom seemed to be smiling more than usual when they greeted them.

Lying on their stomachs, side by side on a large rug, they watched as people watched them. Molly pushed her sunglasses onto her head and turned to look at Ryan, beside her. His eyes had closed, long lashes dark against his tanned skin. 'I had never realised we were so all-fired interesting, had you?'

He didn't open his eyes, but with his head turned towards her as it was he didn't have to raise his voice above a conspirator's whisper. 'We've always been interesting. We just didn't notice it so much before.'

'Doesn't it bother you now that you know?'

'You've been away. I've had this kind of attention and speculation aimed at me ever since I came back here. That's what comes of being single in a small town. You can't so much as say hello to a pretty female without the gossips starting. They've got nothing else to do.'

The wheels turned slowly in her head.

Ryan smiled a slow, sleepy smile, still with his eyes closed. 'Okay, I can hear those wheels a-turnin'. What?'

She hated the way he could do that. What was he? Psychic?

'Haven't you dated anyone since I've been away?'

'Why?' The smile transformed to a grin. 'Jealous?'

'Ha, ha.' She nudged him with her elbow. 'No, I mean, well, you can't *not* have dated anyone since you moved up here. So I guess what I mean is—I'm not cramping your style, am I? Living with you, I mean?'

He opened his eyes and squinted up at her, curious as to what her face might tell him. But she turned away before he could see anything, studying the crowd who lined the shore.

'Moll, if you're asking me whether or not your living in my house is affecting my sex-life, then I think we're about to hit uncharted territory here.'

'Well, we've always been up-front with each other, and half the population already seems to believe I *am* your sex-life. So I was just curious.' She shrugged her shoulders. 'I wondered, that's all.'

Ryan turned onto his side, propping himself up on an elbow to study her closer. He was rewarded for his moment's patience when she turned to look at him. There was concern in her eyes, and he realised she was genuinely worried about 'cramping his style'. Without thinking about it he reached out to her, brushing a long lock of damp auburn hair away from her cheek. 'Even if I was seeing someone, which we both know I'm not—unless, of course, you count *you*—I wouldn't be able to make love to them in the house while you were there.'

Molly noted the quiet affection in his voice and smiled down at him. He really was just such a nice guy. Still, she couldn't resist teasing him. 'What's wrong? You make too much noise?'

His eyes widened in surprise at the jibe. Recognising the teasing light in her eyes, he knew he had no choice but to reply in kind. 'Baby…' he blew onto his fingernails before polishing them on his T-shirt '…it wouldn't be *me* making the noise.'

Molly erupted into convulsive laughter. 'You complete great arrogant lump!'

They laughed together for a moment before watching the crowd again in companionable silence. Ryan thought about the conversation. 'So if you met someone, and the situation was reversed, would I cramp *your* style?'

'Make love with someone while you were in the same house?' She blushed a fiery red and laughed again. 'No way, José.'

'You make too much noise, right?' The question did things to his imagination that it had absolutely no right doing.

She hid her face in the blanket while he watched her shoulders shake with laughter. Her voice was muffled when she eventually spoke, forcing him to lean towards her to hear her words. 'I don't think I could concentrate on what I was doing if I thought you could hear anything.'

Jealousy, like a bad cramp, gripped his chest hard, shocking him with its intensity. Thinking of Molly in that way had always been off limits. Now their conversation had opened a doorway he hadn't intended looking through, and he didn't much care for his reaction.

Clearing his throat, he sprang to his feet and peeled off

his T-shirt. 'Just as well Molly, 'cos whoever he was I think I'd probably be forced to deck him.' He frowned as he looked towards the water. 'I'm going for another swim. See you in a while.'

Molly's head shot upwards at his sharp announcement. But she only focused her vision in time to see him walk briskly to the end of the nearest pier before diving smoothly into the cool water. Where had that outburst come from? She knew he could be protective, but even so...

Their relationship was changing. She sighed as she realised the simple fact of it. It hadn't been the same since she'd come home. She'd begun to realise that when she had noticed Ryan staring at her so often of late. It was as if he'd never really looked at her before, or as if he'd noticed something that he hadn't seen before. She wondered what it was?

And these last few days they had walked onto very new ground; she supposed it was only natural they'd need time to adjust. Time to find and test the new boundaries. But they cared about each other in ways in which she, certainly, had never cared about anyone else. Ryan was her most special of friends, and no matter what adjustments they made she knew they wouldn't—couldn't—affect that attachment. They just couldn't.

'Someone as lovely as you shouldn't frown like that.'

Turning onto her back, she looked up into Nick Scallon's smiling face. Dressed in a pristine white T-shirt and khaki shorts, he resembled a model from the pages of a summer catalogue.

'I'll keep that in mind.' She smiled. 'It's nice to see you again. How are you?'

'I'm just grand.' His blue eyes moved down over her body and her long legs before returning to her face. 'You should wear a swimsuit all the time, Molly. Wow.'

She sat upright, unconsciously drawing her knees up as she glanced towards the lough.

'He's still in the water.'

'Who is?' She blinked at him.

Nick smiled. 'Your *friend* the Park Ranger.'

She glanced back towards the water. 'Oh, you mean Ryan. Yeah, he likes the water. We had swim races here every summer as kids.'

He crouched beside her, taking a deep breath. 'There's a lot of history between you two.'

She looked at his face, surprised to find him so close. 'We've known each other a long time. Yeah, we're close.'

A quick glance over his head caused her to smile at the look of disapproval on Mrs Collins' face. 'In fact I think you'll find your sitting here is setting quite a few tongues wagging.'

He didn't look too worried. 'Your Ryan is well liked in this community. How can I possibly compete with that?'

'From what I hear, a guy like you doesn't let a little matter of competition get in his way.' The words were out before she could stop them. But the minute she spoke Nick's chin dropped, and Molly regretted the innuendo.

'I'm sorry. That was uncalled for. I've always considered a person innocent until proven guilty. I guess I shouldn't treat you any differently.'

'Molly—' He reached out, touching her arm with one long finger, then running the palm of his hand towards her shoulder as he held her gaze with his. 'I—'

'I believe you're occupying my space!'

CHAPTER THREE

THEIR heads snapped upwards in unison as Ryan's shadow fell over them. For a moment Molly didn't recognise him any more quickly than she had recognised the tone of his voice. His face was dark—threatening, almost—and for a split second she was shocked. It was a side to him she didn't see very often. Her conscious mind had never identified him as an alpha male.

'Ryan—sorry. I didn't see you there.' Nick quickly removed his hand from Molly's arm and stood up. 'I was just saying how great Molly looks in a swimsuit.'

Ryan stepped closer to Nick, water running off his body in long silvery rivulets. He ran his hand across his face to remove some of the water and then lowered his voice. 'So I saw, Scallon. The next time you decide to compliment her with your hands you'll have me to deal with—do you understand?'

Molly jumped to her feet and stood between them, facing Ryan. 'Have you gone nuts? Apologise to Nick this minute.'

Nick smiled smoothly, his eyes warming for Molly. 'It's okay, Molly, I understand.' His eyes swept back towards Ryan. 'Ryan obviously feels the need to stake his claim. I get the message.'

Ryan nodded tersely. 'Just make sure you do.'

Molly gaped at the two men. 'Oh, you two can't be for real.'

Ignoring Nick for a moment, Ryan frowned at Molly.

'This guy was *touching* you. Are you telling me that's okay with you? Because it sure as hell isn't okay with me!'

Without hesitating she grabbed his hand and tugged him away from Nick, towards the trees at the back of the shore-line. 'We need to talk, *now*.'

By the time they reached the trees Ryan was smiling at her. 'Wow, you can drag me into the trees any time, Moll. Did you see the looks we got?'

'What the hell were you doing out there?'

She was mad—really, really mad. He could tell. Her green eyes sparked angrily and her face was flushed. He thought she looked amazing.

'We're supposed to be a couple, right? Well, I'm not going to stand by while some other man runs his hands all over my girlfriend, now, am I?'

Molly shook her head. 'Even as my boyfriend, or for that matter as my lover, you wouldn't go around acting like Neanderthal man without my going crazy about it. Don't you know that?' She glared at him. 'What the heck kind of woman have you been dating over the years?'

He actually had the grace to look apologetic. 'I'm sorry. I just—well, I guess I didn't like it much. As a friend *or* as a boyfriend.'

Realising she still held his hand, he squeezed her fingers. 'I guess we've both got some learning to do if we're going to pull this off.'

Calmer, she looked up into his eyes and smiled wryly. 'They're all standing out there watching these trees, aren't they?'

'Yup.'

'So what'll we do? Wait for a minute?'

Ryan took a deep breath. 'They'll probably expect us to kiss and make up first.'

'Oh.'

He stepped towards her. 'And we should probably practise that kissing thing again before we try it out in public, right? After all, they'll expect you to come out of here looking like you've just been thoroughly kissed, and the best way I know to make you look like that is...'

Molly interrupted him, suddenly terribly aware of how little clothing he was wearing. Her mouth was dry. 'I get the gist, Callaghan. So you'd better just shut up and kiss me, then.'

'And they say romance is dead.'

This time Molly was ready for his kiss. She even moistened her lips automatically before his head lowered. *It's only Ryan, only Ryan, only Ryan.* She echoed it over and over in her head, but after a moment it was hard to concentrate.

When he felt her kiss him back it shocked him. He didn't know what he'd expected, but he certainly wasn't ready for how hot she felt, how easily their mouths fitted together. With a kiss there was always that initial moment of hesitation as the two parties felt for the correct 'fit' before they deepened the kiss. But not this time. This was right from the first touch.

Moving instinctively, she loosened her hand and wound her arms around his neck, reaching up to pull herself closer to his damp body. Ryan's arms in turn circled her waist to hold her there. Her curved body fitted along the full length of his, curling in and touching him everywhere.

The minute his tongue touched hers she was lost, and stopped thinking at all. In her entire life she couldn't remember being kissed so thoroughly—and by Ryan, of all people!

By Ryan. She froze. Oh, no, this couldn't be happening. She couldn't possibly be enjoying kissing *Ryan.* It wasn't something that was supposed to happen when you kissed a friend.

The moment she went still he knew they'd gone too far. Whatever was happening it was too much. He carefully pulled away and stepped back, taking a moment before he could look at her.

Molly, in turn, was staring at him with large unblinking eyes, as if she'd never seen him before. Her lips were red and swollen, her cheeks flushed. She was beautiful. When had she got so beautiful? All of a sudden he realised that was what was different about her since she'd been home. She'd grown and matured into a very beautiful woman and he hadn't allowed himself to realise it. Until then.

He smiled softly at her. 'I think they'll know what we've been doing when we go out there.'

Turning away from him, Molly found her voice. 'Well, thank goodness *someone* knows what we're doing.'

By the following weekend Molly's nerves were shot to hell and back. The whole town was talking about the wonderful romance between Ryan Callaghan and that 'pretty wee O'Brien girl'. And Nick Scallon had been to visit her again in the shop.

Things weren't quite going the way she had expected— not that she'd known what to expect in the first place. And then there was Kate. Kate, whom she saw every day and who quizzed her every moment possible.

Saturday proved to be no different.

'So, how's it going, then?'

Molly sighed and shook her head. 'You ask me this every day, and every day I tell you the same thing—*fine*.'

Kate sat down beside her and looked her in the face. 'If it were going fine you wouldn't look this bad. You look exhausted, Molly, and you can't keep telling me it's ''fine'' and look so unhappy. Aren't things working out between you and Ryan?'

'No, it's not that. It's just—' She struggled to find an excuse and couldn't. Not this time. 'I'm confused, I guess.'

'About you and Ryan, or about Nick Scallon?'

Molly laughed tightly. 'I thought I liked Nick Scallon but I was wrong about that. The more I see of him the more—I don't know—*smarmy* I find him.'

'Mmm. He is a bit too slick, if you ask me.' Kate smiled sympathetically and rubbed her friend's arm. 'And Ryan?'

'Now, there's a whole 'nother story.' Her fingers rubbed her temples. 'Where should I begin?'

'He kiss you again?'

Did he ever. 'Oh, yeah. He did that all right.'

Kate smiled broadly. 'Good grief. And you just don't know what to do about that, do you?'

Now, there was an understatement. Even without the whole story, as usual, Kate was close to the mark. 'We're not the same any more, and I hate that. I miss the fun we used to have. I just don't know how to get it back.'

'On a scale of one to ten?'

Molly looked confused. 'What?'

'On a scale of one to ten, how did the kiss rate?'

'If you're going to make fun I'm leaving, Kate, I swear.'

Kate shook her head. 'No, I'm completely serious. I need to know how you rated the kiss. It gives me an idea of the scale of your problem. Anyway, you can't leave. It's your shop too.'

Molly blinked at her friend in amazement, then shrugged her shoulders and thought for a moment. *On a scale of one to ten.* She'd thought about their last kiss far too much over sleepless nights, so it didn't take long to rate. Her tone was as deadpan as her face when she spoke.

'About fifteen.'

'Damn it, I just always thought it would be.'

'Kate! This isn't helping.'

'Sorry.' She looked more serious. 'You ever been kissed above an eight before?'

Deadpan again. 'No.'

'So now you've got the oldest of problems to deal with here. Do you chance losing your friendship for what will probably be the most amazing lovemaking of your life? Or do you hang onto the friendship with it possibly never being the same again because you always wonder whether it would have been the best lovemaking of your life?'

'Correct me if that's not a lose/lose situation you just quoted there, Oprah. I thought you were supposed to be helping.'

Kate nodded. 'I am. I was just thinking out loud. In fact, here's another. Do you love him?'

'What did you say?' Molly couldn't believe what she'd just been asked. 'Did you just ask me if I *love* him? What the hell kind of question is that? It's Ryan we're discussing here, not some guy I've just been out on a blind date with!'

Kate held her hands up in front of her. 'Okay, okay, calm down. I know you care about him; I've always known that. You were like some loyal terrier when you first found out I had a crush on him. What I mean is do you *love him* love him. You know—the big one.'

'Don't be ridiculous. He's kissed me twice and you expect me to fall head over heels? It's Ryan. I can't fall in love with Ryan. It would be like—hell I don't know—like falling in love with a big brother.'

'Ryan's not your brother, Molly.' Kate walked over and hugged her friend as best she could with eight months' worth of baby in the way. 'You want my advice? You go with the flow and let things happen naturally. If you two are meant to be together then there's nothing you can do to stop that except lie to yourself. He's a great fella, Molly, and if you're not meant to be then it's the biggest test of your friendship you'll ever have. All friendships have to change and grow, and when you think about it it would change when you marry other partners anyway. So just wait and see, and stop killing yourself over this.'

The words echoed through Molly's head and she wondered what Kate would think if she knew the whole story. It was a bit difficult to let things happen naturally when everything they were doing was such a lie to begin with.

She had never for one moment expected that their dumbass bet would be so testing, or so dangerous. But then how could she have possibly known that kissing him would have such an effect on her?

There was a chance that the forfeit for this dare could be larger than she wanted to pay. She could lose her very best friend, for ever.

After the party—twelve years ago

He was sick of dating bimbos. It was the only type of girl he seemed to spend any time with these days and he was bored. Bored and out of sorts. Ever since Molly's birthday party.

It was just that at least if he was dating someone he could cover up the fact that he was obsessed with Molly's relationship with Kieran. It wasn't natural, this sudden realisation he had about Molly O'Brien being an attractive, sexy female. As if these twenty-one-year-old hormones weren't enough to be dealing with. No. He had to take it one step further. His nether regions reacted every time his best friend walked past. Great plan.

But it wasn't just his newfound realisation of how she looked. Not if he was honest with himself. It was the fact that she had less time for him now that she was seeing Kieran. Before they had always talked on the phone, or written, but now she talked on the phone to *Kieran* and sent notes to *Kieran*. It was only natural. But Ryan was jealous as hell.

'Hey, stranger.' The voice sounded close to his ear, making him jerk with surprise. Turning round, he was met with a familiar smile and an immediate hug. Great. Now all he had to do was think about her and she appeared. That would help.

'What are you doing here?'

'Well, that's some welcome, I must say.' She sat down on the wide edge of his father's desk. 'Remind me to visit you more often.'

Immediately Ryan felt guilty. It wasn't her fault he was an immature prat. It was up to him to try and control himself more. After all, she wasn't some possession of his. He wasn't her keeper. Who was he to deny her any touch of happiness she could find? And he guessed if she had to spend time with someone else then he was glad it was his other best friend. Kieran was a good guy. He knew that. And surely playing the martyr was a much better feeling than playing the wounded party?

'It's just you don't normally come down here, O'Brien, that's all.' He waved a hand around his father's office. 'It's the one place I'm normally safe from you.'

Molly raised an eyebrow, then stuck her tongue out at him. 'Pig.'

'Yep, that's me.' He glanced down at her white shirt and tracksuit bottoms, and the racquet at her feet. 'Off to enter Wimbledon, are we?'

'Something like that. I'll just wait and see if I manage to beat Kieran in another game first.'

'Ah.' Ryan turned back to his filing cabinet. 'So you're playing next door at the club?'

Molly studied the back of his head. Either it was her paranoia or Ryan's tone was cold. She had been noticing a change in him recently. 'What's up, Callaghan?'

Now, there was a loaded question these days. He smiled wryly. 'Why on earth should you ask that?'

'It's just…' She thought for a moment. 'Have I done something to annoy you?'

'Any more than usual?'

She smiled at his back. 'Yeah, any more than usual. It's just you're not yourself at the minute.'

Ryan tried for the second time to file an invoice correctly.

There was silence for a moment as the wheels turned in Molly's head. She knew she'd been spending a lot of time with Kieran and less time with her best friend. But that was natural, wasn't it? Ever since Kieran had come on holiday with Ryan the previous summer she'd been obsessed with him. And now he was hers. But had she hurt Ryan's feelings by spending less time with him?

'Have I been ignoring you?'

Ryan took a deep breath and turned round again. He noted the look in her eye, the concern. He felt lower than a rat's behind. 'It's okay. You're crazy about that stupid friend of mine and, believe me, he has my sympathy.' He smiled encouragingly.

'It's just I can't remember the last time we talked.'

'We talked yesterday.'

'I said hi before you put Kieran on the phone. It's hardly the same thing.'

The filing cabinet drawer closed as he leaned back, folding his arms across his chest. 'Okay, so what do you want to know?'

'How's life, Callaghan? Still dating the lovely Susie?' She fluttered her eyelashes at him.

It drew the required laughter. 'She has her good points.'

Mmm.' Molly's eyebrows arched again. 'I've noticed that most boys spend their time talking to two of those "good points".'

'Jealousy, jealousy.'

She glanced down at her chest. 'Well, they do say anything more than a handful is a waste.'

Ryan laughed. 'Where do you get this smutty talk?'

'Why, from you, of course.'

'I have never said that to you!'

'No.' She blinked innocently up at him. 'But you said it to Kieran about that girl in the bar a couple of weeks ago.'

'Eavesdroppers never hear any good, y'know.'

Molly smiled. 'Maybe. So, anyway, is she wifey material? 'Cos you know you'd better get a move on if you're going to have those twelve children before the deadline.'

He smiled at the memory of an old dare, when Molly had bet he'd be married with twelve kids by the time he turned thirty. Married and settled into his family's business. Just as his parents had always planned. Looking away, he returned to his filing. 'I don't think so.'

'Well, you better keep lookin' if you're going to produce a son and heir for this dynasty of yours.'

'Yeah, well, I hardly think it's a dynasty.'

Molly persisted. 'Aw, c'mon, Callaghan. Everywhere I look these days a house is being built by Callaghan and Son.'

'Business is good.'

Even though she was reflecting on how much nicer Ryan's hair was short, Molly still managed to notice the chill in his voice. 'Okay, this would be a bad thing because…?'

Another sigh. 'I don't want it, Moll.'

His words silenced her. Momentarily.

'You're kidding?'

'God, I wish I was.'

Molly stared at his back. 'Look at me.'

Slowly, very slowly, he turned to face her. Shoving his clenched fists into his pockets he looked into her eyes. 'I thought you of all people might have known.'

She shook her head. 'Not a clue. But you're doing that whole business management course and all. Why do that if you aren't getting ready for all this?'

'I guess I thought it would make my dad happy.' He shook his head. 'You should see his face when he talks about Callaghan and Son. He's worked his whole life for this.'

Molly's heart wrenched for him. 'Oh, God, what will you do?'

A smile. 'You know something? I haven't got a clue.'

'You have to tell him.'

'How?' The smile disappeared.

Silence.

'You see, you don't know either.' He turned back to his filing. 'I'll just stay here until I wither up and die from terminal boredom.'

Molly knew how much Ryan loved his family. She knew how honest, open and loyal he was with them. Her own parents had often teased him about being the perfect child. And in many ways he was.

His parents had waited a long time for him, and he spent most of his life rewarding them for their patience. She couldn't remember a time when there had been anything but pride in their eyes when they looked at him. So it was no great surprise that he would do just about anything not to hurt or disappoint them. He was the nicest person she knew. Her heart twisted for him.

Ryan heard her soft movements as she walked over to him. Felt the warmth of her small hand as it rested on his shoulder. He turned to look at her.

'They wouldn't want you to spend your life doing something that made you miserable.'

'And throwing their lives' work back at them won't make *them* miserable, right?'

Molly put her arms around his waist and hugged him. 'They *love* you; they'll get over it. You need to find out what you're meant to do with your own life.'

Ryan hesitated for a moment before wrapping his arms around her to return the hug. 'I just can't hurt them, Moll. It means too much.'

She lifted her head from his chest and looked up into his stormy eyes. 'This will work out. You wait and see. Just don't lie to yourself about it. It's not you. You're the most honest person I know.'

He stared down into her shimmering eyes. Molly was so special to him. She was the only person he could have told his secret to. He knew she'd stand by him, no matter what he decided to do, and he loved her for it. All these feelings he'd been having were just hormones. That was all. At his stage of life he couldn't look at any attractive female without having some sort of a reaction. That was all it was. Chemistry. Just chemistry. What he already had with this 'kid sister' of his was all that mattered.

Molly's rat was winning the race. She squealed in delight as it made its way down the plastic runway to its piece of food a split second before Ryan's.

'I don't believe it,' Ryan muttered over her shoulder.

'What do you do? Study rat racing form, or something? How many's that you've won now?'

She grinned back at him. 'Four. Count 'em and weep.'

'You know the trainer, don't you?'

'Yeah, sure, that's it, Callaghan.' Trying her best to keep a straight face, she blinked. 'I scout round all the rat trainers' homes, studying form, so that I can make that all-important fifty-cent bet. It's how I make a living, you know.'

He poked her in the ribs with one long finger. 'Well, in that case it's your round.' One hand gently pushing against the small of her back, he guided her towards the table where Kate and her husband Paul were waiting. 'Just try to remember your friends when you're rich and famous.'

Molly slid onto the seat beside Kate and grinned widely. 'Callaghan's getting thrashed and he's hating it.'

He leaned over her head. 'You know what they say— Lucky in rat racing, unlucky in love. Which is why even when I lose, I win.'

He winked, then kissed the top of Molly's head.

Kate laughed at their easy bantering. 'You two just never stop, do you? I don't think I can remember a time when you weren't this double act that everyone outside watches with fascination.'

'But wasn't the rest nice when she was away?'

'Ryan! That's awful. You know rightly we all missed her.'

Molly elbowed him lightly in the stomach, grinning when he overreacted at the 'pain'. 'Some people just don't appreciate their nearest and dearest. He'd miss me if I went back, just you ask him.'

She glanced up at him from the edge of her eyes. Looking down at her, he seemed to ponder something for a moment, and a variety of emotions flickered across his expressive eyes. Then he nodded. 'I'd miss you even more than I missed you before.'

They stared at each other, then Ryan smiled over at Kate. 'That's about the slushiest stuff you're getting outta me tonight, gang. Anyone want anything from the bar?'

Paul accompanied him as he left the table; Molly's and Kate's eyes followed them as they left. Then Kate smiled at her friend. 'Well, things look okay with you two tonight. You had a talk, then?'

'Nope.' They'd hardly had time to speak at all in the rush to change after work, then get to Riley's Bar for the first night of the town's festival activities. 'But you're right. We are having fun tonight. It's the kind of silly, fun thing we're used to. Having you guys here is helping too.'

'He did, you know.' Kate sipped at her soft drink. 'Miss you, I mean. A blind man could have seen it.'

Molly studied him from a distance. 'You think?'

'Oh, yes. He was seriously good at his work, mind you. Things wouldn't run as smoothly out there now if it hadn't been for all his organising. But he wasn't the same fella he is now.'

'Really?'

Kate shook her head. 'Come on, now, don't tell me you're not interested in what was happening while you were away. You spoke to him in those six years, didn't you?'

A nod. There had been letters, more sporadic as the years went on and they had both become busy with their lives. But they had still written to each other. And spoken too— calls at Christmas and birthdays. She might have been on the other side of the world but Molly had never forgotten where she came from, her family, or the people dearest to her. It was part of the reason that she had eventually felt the calling to come home.

'Okay, so what did I miss, then?' She turned to look at her friend. 'He never did get round to telling me about any mad affairs that he had.'

Kate tilted her head slightly, examining Molly's face. 'You don't honestly think he was a hermit, do you?'

Her eyes were drawn back to the bar. 'No. I guess I never really thought about it.'

'Because you didn't think of him in that way, right?'

'I guess.'

'And now?'

She sighed? She did want to know. 'Okay, I'll bite. Who was he seeing while I was away?'

'Well, there were a few girls that tried it on on the odd night out, like this. I think Marie Donnelly even managed a kiss or two one New Year's Eve.'

Molly thought a moment, a frown creasing her forehead. 'There were a few in Dublin. I know he saw one of them for nearly a year in his early twenties, 'cos we gave him powerful stick about it.'

'What was she like?'

'Gorgeous, in a plastic doll kinda way.'

'A bit like Maura, then.' Kate nodded to the bar.

Molly looked round to witness Maura pushing her very visible cleavage towards Ryan's chest as she looked up at him from beneath long lashes. Swallowing the remainder of the wine in her glass in one mouthful, Molly glanced at Kate and smiled. 'Excuse me. I think I need to be somewhere.'

Laughter followed her from the table. 'Go get her, girl!'

CHAPTER FOUR

RYAN was actually smiling back at Maura by the time Molly got to him. The bare-faced cheek of the woman, muscling in when he was Molly's guy. Half the town knew that, for goodness' sake.

Moving in close, Molly slipped her arm around his waist and snuggled into his side. She smiled sweetly at him, reaching across Maura's chest to lift her wine glass from the bar. 'This would be mine, then.'

Maura stepped back, her eyes narrowing at the innuendo. 'Well, Molly, how nice. I was just saying how good it is to see everyone out for my festival events.'

Sitting on as many committees as possible was one of Maura's many hobbies, and she revelled in the glory of playing hostess. Molly glanced down over her scoop-neck sweater and tight-fitting trousers, and immediately felt under-dressed and dowdy.

'Molly's been winning on the races, haven't you?' Following her lead, Ryan moved his arm to circle her waist, holding her close to him. 'I'm hoping she'll earn enough to keep me into my old age.'

'Why, Ryan, now, a man in his prime shouldn't be thinking about old age. You should be thinking about having fun.'

Molly lifted her new wine glass from the bar, telling herself that if she threw the contents over Maura's sweater it would probably leave a stain. Shame, that. But still.

'Oh, I think we can manage to arrange to have some fun—don't you *Ryan*?'

Ryan balked at the use of his name. He was so used to Molly calling him Callaghan that it caught him off guard. That and the fact that she had just turned against him and managed to press her breasts against his side. Man, when she played dirty, she played dirty. He glanced down at where she was touching him and was rewarded with a brief glimpse of flesh at the V-neck of her cream shirt. Swallowing, he looked into her eyes. 'You have something in mind, do you, Moll?'

She raised her chin and looked him straight in the eyes, smiling seductively. 'Why don't we discuss that later, at *home*?'

Ryan's mouth went dry. Dear Lord, when had she learned to do that? He could remember Molly being plenty of things over the years, but he'd never before seen her as a seductress. At least, not up close. Now all of a sudden he was noticing far too many things about her that he had entirely no business noticing. Clearing his throat, he smiled weakly at Maura. Looking at her seemed safer for the moment, and maybe if he talked to her he could take his mind off what Molly was doing to his libido.

'Well, there you go. Never a dull moment with Molly.' He managed a laugh, reaching for his beer in desperation. 'You can see she keeps me occupied, Maura.'

Maura remained cool, her eyes boring into Molly before returning to soften at Ryan. 'It's as well I know you two so well or I might start to believe all these rumours about you. But your relationship has always seemed a bit unnatural to me, so I know this is only some little game you're playing. That's all right.' She waved across the room. 'I can wait. I know that whatever it is you're doing won't last long.'

Molly leaned towards her. 'I wouldn't hold my breath if I were you, Maura. What's mine is mine. And believe me,

after being with me, everything else will always seem…'
She let her eyes wander down and then up again over
Maura's slim figure. 'Let's just say, *wanting* in some areas.'

The woman positively bristled as she smiled at Ryan,
then walked away. Molly turned to face him. Setting her
drink back on the bar, she put both hands around his waist,
linking her thumbs under the belt loops in his jeans. Then
she moved in close, raising her chin to smile at him. Her
voice was low. 'How am I doing, then?'

Dark eyes stared at her for a moment, and then he
laughed.

He leaned back to rest against the bar, looping his fingers
together in the small of her back. 'You, my old friend, are
a scary woman.'

'Am I, now?' She laughed. 'So, tell me, do I scare you
too?'

He raised his eyes heavenwards, taking a deep breath.
'Right this minute you do. You're much better at this than
I'd thought you'd be.'

Molly realised he was blushing when he looked at her
again. 'I'm your *girlfriend*, remember? What way did you
think I'd be?'

'I don't know what I thought you'd be like as a girlfriend. I just didn't expect to be—' He looked into the air
for the right words. What was the point in trying to lie?
She knew him too well for that. And he was *really* bad at
lying. 'I hadn't expected to be *affected* by the things you
do.'

With a similar sigh Molly leaned her forehead against
his chest for a moment before looking up at him again.
Honesty. Thank goodness for that. She had been wondering
if they'd managed to lose that quality to their relationship
altogether. 'Since we're actually managing to discuss this,

I think I need to know where the heck did you learn to kiss the way you do?'

He looked confused. 'You lost me. Kiss like what?'

'Like—' Molly blushed. 'Well, you kiss good, that's all.'

That raised a proud smirk. 'Thanks.'

She laughed. 'This is the craziest thing we've ever done.'

'Possibly.' He tugged her closer to him, looking down into her eyes. 'But then you have to admit I *have* saved you from the attentions of Mr Smarmy. You ready to admit yet that I was right about him?'

They both knew that Nick had visited and tried calling her. Molly just hadn't quite got round to admitting that there might have been something in Ryan's words to begin with. After all, she had been fairly distracted by other things recently.

'If I do, then do we "break up" early?'

Ryan's eyes studied her face. 'Is that what you want to do?'

'Break up with you?' Her laughter was nervous. 'Well, that was always the plan, right?'

One dark eyebrow raised in question. 'What's up, O'Brien? You scared to see this through to the end?' He leaned towards her, his voice low. 'Challenge too much for you?'

Her smile was slow as she stood on tiptoes and kissed his smooth shaven cheek. She breathed in the familiar musky scent of his aftershave, taking time to choose her words. When she spoke, her voice was low, her breath tickling against his ear. 'Callaghan, I'm not going anywhere. We said three months, and I intend to torture you for every second of that time.'

Ryan's face broke into a wide smile, his relief at her words almost palpable. He hadn't realised how much he wanted to continue the pretence. Maybe he should have examined that feeling more closely, but Molly chose that moment to snuggle her head beneath his chin, distracting him again.

She moved her hands from his waistband to run her palms along his back while she listened to the thud of his heart beneath her ear. 'Just you let me know when you've had enough.'

Ten years ago

Molly's heart was breaking for him.

Her chest twisted painfully, her throat constricting so tightly that it was almost impossible to breathe. 'I'm so sorry.' Her voice caught on the words.

Ryan remained still, his bloodshot eyes focused on the rain running in wide rivulets down the window pane.

Molly reached a shaky hand towards him, hesitated, then touched his arm. She waited a second and then squeezed her fingers gently. A harsh gust of wind blew the rain harder against the window. Ryan stared.

'Callaghan?'

His jaw clenched and unclenched. She squeezed his arm again. Felt the tightly held control he was exerting over his emotions. 'Ryan, please.'

With unbearable slowness he turned towards her. 'I can't do this now.'

'Do what?'

His eyes searched hers. 'Watch you grieve too.'

A sob escaped from her throat. 'I won't leave you.'

'O'Brien—'

Molly stepped in closer and wrapped her arms around his waist. Laying her cheek against his chest, she could feel the tension in his body. 'No, Callaghan, not this time.' She lifted her head to look up into his face. 'Don't you see? You need me now.'

He blinked at her, his jaw clenching again. 'Don't you know that if I let you stay I might not want to ever let go? You're all I have left now.'

The tears spilled over onto her cheeks. 'That's what friends are for. The good times and the bad.' She smiled sadly. 'I won't ever leave you.'

'I want them back, Moll.' His deep voice caught on the words, his arms closing around her. 'I never got to say everything I wanted to say.'

'They knew.' Her long fingers stroked his hair back. 'You didn't need to say the words.'

A tear escaped from the corner of his eye. 'I can never seem to say what I really feel, Molly. And people deserve that.'

Molly cried with him. 'Then tell them now. They're listening. And I'll be right here with you. I love you.'

Two and a half years later

He'd gone a little crazy for a while after his parents died. It was natural, Molly supposed, now she had the benefit of hindsight.

'You're trying to get yourself killed? Is that what this is about?'

He looked down at the wildcat below him. Molly was madder than hell, and probably with due cause.

'Is that what it's going to take, Callaghan? You won't rest until I have to go identify your body somewhere! Well, you know what?' She stood on her tiptoes to push her nose into his face. 'Go right ahead. I can't do this any more.'

Ryan watched with dark eyes as she stormed away from him. She didn't mean it; he knew that much. He knew she'd been hurting just as much as he had since his parents had gone. Maybe even more, because she'd absorbed some of his pain too. After a moment he turned to look at Kieran. 'I'm in big trouble over this, aren't I?'

His friend nodded. 'Oh, yeah. Deeply in the smelly stuff.'

'Thought so.'

They watched her departing figure until it was out of sight. Ryan sighed. 'You think I've got a death wish too, Kieran?'

Kieran's grey eyes were thoughtful for a minute. He scratched his chin with one long finger while he thought, and then he smiled. 'I think you fight really hard and risk your skin for things you probably can't change.'

Ryan huffed. 'Well, someone has to try and do something. If it weren't for volunteers in some of these places then those animals would be extinct by now.'

'So you're going to single-handedly save the entire planet?'

A grin. 'I can try.'

Kieran shook his head. 'No wonder she's given up on you.'

'She only thinks she has.'

'Beer?'

Ryan threw an arm across his friend's shoulders. 'Now I know *someone* loves me!'

They wandered towards the airport bar and settled down into a booth while waiting for their drinks. Ryan closed his eyes as the cooling liquid slid down his throat. Boy, but he'd missed real beer.

'So what now, Ryan?' Kieran eyed him over the neck of

his bottle. 'Another crusade that will make my home-life hell for a few months?'

It had been six months since Kieran and Molly had set up home. Something that, at the time, had amused Ryan greatly. 'One step closer to those twelve kids,' he'd teased.

'Don't hold your breath,' she'd retorted.

But he had worried at the time—needlessly, as it turned out. They were his friends, and he cared about them both. But Molly was different. In all the world there was no one else he cared as much for. Not since his parents had died. She was his family now. The one person he knew would love him regardless of the stupid things he did. He would always look out for her, first and foremost.

Kieran was another story. There was just something—different about him. He wasn't as open and carefree as he'd been back in their university days. Almost as if he'd lost something in his transition to adulthood. But then, Ryan was hardly the same person he had been three years ago. And neither, he supposed, was Molly. That was just life, after all, right? People changed. Things that happened in their lives changed them. It was just that he'd been so absorbed in his own problems he'd lost touch with his friends and their lives. An oversight that he had been thinking about only too recently. And one that he intended to rectify.

Still, the thought that his escapades nearly always had a knock-on effect on their home-life amused him for a few moments. 'Still takes stuff out on you when she's annoyed at me, huh?'

Kieran drew a deep breath. 'Ooh, yeah. It's my fault for not keeping you out of trouble, y'know.'

'Damn right too.'

They took a moment to savour their drinks, then Kieran asked, 'Is it helping any, Ryan?'

Ryan looked down at his drink. 'Is what helping?'

'All this running away.'

He scratched his new growth of beard for a moment. Not too much time for shaving when you were trying to catch poachers. Before that it had been fighting off construction crews outside the rainforests. Before that it had been volunteer work on a Greenpeace ship. All the money he'd made from the sale of his father's construction company had helped fund his personal crusade, with plenty to spare. But was it enough? Was he any less lonely or empty? Did he hurt any less now than he had two and a half years ago?

'No, not really.'

They drank some more and then ordered again. Ryan sighed. 'Look, I'm sorry if my running around has caused Molly any pain.'

Kieran shrugged his shoulders. 'Not me you need to say that to.'

He nodded. 'Yeah. I'll tell her.'

Kieran looked him straight in the eye. 'Where now, then? You stayin' a while or is this a flying visit before you go save something else?'

'No, I've done my bit for a while.' He smiled at the sceptical sidelong glance. 'I'm serious. I had some time to think on this trip.'

Laughter. 'Yeah—now, you see, a hospital stay will do that.'

Ryan grimaced. 'It was a *flesh wound*. It's not like I lost a limb. I just got to lie around and think for a while, that's all.'

'The only problem with the idea of a flesh wound is that Molly is smart enough to understand it goes hand in hand with the fact that someone shot at you.'

Another grimace. 'You see, now, that'll get ya' thinkin'.'

'I bet.'

They drank some more.

'I want to come home, Kieran.'

'Home to where?'

Ryan had sold the house too. Nothing was left to remind him of what he'd lost. In the haze of hurt that surrounded the car accident he'd done everything he could to tidy things away. He smiled. 'I thought I'd go to Boyle and live in the summer house for a while.'

'More ghosts?'

'Maybe.' He raised his bottle to his mouth. 'But the best kind of ones. I always seem to have been happy there.'

The day after the rat races dawned bright and warm, with a more optimistic air in the Callaghan household. Molly slept in, lazed around in her towelling robe while reading the newspapers, then fed Houdini. A perfect, lazy Sunday morning.

Ryan had held her hand on the walk home while they'd talked and joked just as they always did. He'd even dared her to enter the festival's Lady of the Lake pageant—which she'd turned down flat, much to his amusement. So they had debated the merits of beauty pageants over hot chocolate until the wee small hours.

He'd already left to check the park before Molly woke. With the camping and caravanning season upon them, the park staff worked irregular hours. It was part of Ryan's job to co-ordinate it all, and he took it very seriously. Sometimes she was forced to tease him about it. But she knew he wouldn't change his life. And she was proud of him.

Home by lunch, he was smiling and teasing just as normal. 'Hey, there.' Creeping up behind her in the kitchen, he ruffled her hair to distract her while he stole cucumber from her chopping board. 'Thought any more about the beauty contest?'

She slapped his hand away on his second attempt to steal food. 'Nope, and neither will I and you know it. I'm not beauty contest material. We discussed this, remember?'

'Remind me again—something about exploitation and sex discrimination and—nah. I forget the rest.'

Smiling, she turned to look at him and found him a few inches closer than expected. 'Callaghan—'

He closed the gap between them. 'What happened to *Ryan*?'

Her finger poked him in his broad chest. 'You've always been plain old Callaghan to me. You only get your first name when I'm flirting with you for the benefit of other women's eyes.'

'So you were flirting, not trying to *seduce* me?'

'Dream on, big guy.' She stood on tiptoes to move her face closer to his. 'Just 'cos I said you kissed good doesn't mean I'm going to fawn all over you.'

Ryan held his ground. 'How *should* I kiss you to get you to fawn all over me, then?'

That backed her off a little, but with the counter behind her she couldn't go too far. She smiled. 'Oh, no, you don't. The kissing thing is a public thing, remember?'

'So behind the trees at Doon was public, was it?'

'Hell, no, but the idea was there. It was for the benefit of the masses, if you recall?'

'Yes, but that was before you told me that I kissed good.'

She frowned at him. 'Aw, no, you can't go changing the rules of this halfway through. This is play-acting, not reality.'

He reached past her for another slice of cucumber. As his arm brushed the side of her body she jumped, and he grinned. 'Play-acting. Right. So, you thinking I kiss good is play-acting, and the fact that I can't go near you without you going all jumpy is play-acting too?'

Molly was rapidly losing her good mood with his teasing. 'This isn't funny. It's not something you can tease me about—like beauty contests or my calling you names or winning rat races. This is serious stuff.'

'I know.'

The phone rang.

Ryan stared at Molly. She looked nervous and he found his heart beating a little faster than it should be. He needed to talk to her now that he'd had some time away from her to think things over. Honesty. It was what their relationship had always been based on, and he didn't want that to change.

The phone continued ringing. Molly spoke first. 'The phone.'

'I hear it.'

She smiled. 'It's traditional to answer it when it rings.'

'This is true.' He smiled back.

'I'd get it, only there appears to be this *lump* in my way.'

'Really?'

She laughed, placed the palms of her hands against his chest and shoved hard. 'Move, you great oaf and let me get the phone.'

He laughed too, but did eventually move. 'See, you just can't keep your hands off me, can you?'

She was still laughing as she answered the phone. 'Callaghan house.'

'Hey, there, gorgeous.'

Her breath caught in her throat. 'Kieran? Hey, how are you?' A small smile followed. 'We were beginning to think you'd dropped off the face of the planet.'

Laughter. 'No, not so far. You keeping that rebel-without-a-clue in check for me?'

'Believe me—' she looked over at Ryan '—I'm trying.'

'You always were one for a challenge. Anyway, we're about to take him up on that offer of a visit.'

'We?'

'Well, you know you always complain bitterly that it's about time I realised I'm nearly middle-aged and settle down and get married…?'

Molly hesitated, then, 'No!'

She could hear the smile in his voice as he spoke. 'Yeah, you won that bet. Neave said she'd better keep me in line outside the office as well as in it.'

Neave had been his 'girl Friday' for several years, running his chaotic office. Molly had always wondered how long it would take for him to notice how the dark-haired girl looked at him. She knew that look only too well. For a long time it was how she'd looked at him herself.

'Well it's about time.'

'So we'll be there some time tomorrow to see you two, okay?'

'Okay.' She looked at Ryan and frowned. 'We'll see you then.'

'Bye, Molly.'

'Bye.'

She set the phone back in place and turned slowly to look back at Ryan's face. She stared at him for several moments, still frowning.

'What is it? What's wrong?'

'Kieran and Neave got engaged.'

He grinned. 'But that's great, isn't it?' He thought for a moment and then frowned himself. 'Isn't it?'

'You idiot. They're coming *here* to stay for a while!' She turned on her heel and stormed out of the kitchen.

Ryan caught up with her when she hit the porch. 'So what's the problem?'

He tried to push the thought from his mind that said she

wasn't over Kieran yet. The thought twisted in his gut. They had been together for so long and they'd thought they were in love. What if Molly was still in love with him? No. He shook his head to clear his thoughts. She was over him.

'The problem?' She turned and waved her arms out on either side of her body. 'Well, let's just think about that a moment, shall we? We're currently lying to everyone who knows us, half the world thinks we're sleeping together, we haven't a clue how to deal with all this kissing stuff, and now Kieran and his fiancée are coming for a nice, cosy little visit!' There was a dramatic pause as she glared up at him. 'So can *you* tell me how we're going to explain all this?'

Ryan ran his fingers through his dark hair, ruffling it out of place. 'Ah.'

He'd almost said *Would it really matter?* But he'd caught himself in time. That was ridiculous. They both cared about Kieran's feelings. And Ryan wasn't sure how Kieran would react to the idea of him and Molly being together.

'*Ah?* That's all you've got to say? That's great—just great.'

'We'll just have to keep a low profile.'

'And bribe everyone in town not to mention how great it is to see us together?' She placed her hands on her hips. 'Good plan.'

He frowned at her. 'Calm down! All we've got to do is tell them that the rumour merchants have gone over the top and behave like normal. It'll be fine. Hell, Kieran will be so wrapped up in his own news that he'll not even notice us.'

Molly looked at him incredulously. 'How can you say that? How can you say we'll behave like normal when we haven't been ''normal'' since I came home?' She shook her head. 'And we've been nothing even *resembling* normal ever since we started this little charade.'

Her words riled him more than he was prepared for. With a dangerous glint in the depths of his dark eyes, he stepped towards her. 'And why exactly do you think that is, O'Brien?'

'Because, you great thick oaf, we're actually really, genuinely, *physically* attracted to each other. And neither of us knows how to deal with that. That's why!'

'Well, now that's out in the open, what do you suggest we do?'

Molly stared at him, open-mouthed. She couldn't believe she'd actually said it out loud. It was something she hadn't even managed to admit to herself, never mind discussing it with Ryan. But it was the truth.

At some point she'd started to look at Ryan and see a man. Not just plain old Ryan, her friend, but Ryan a member of the opposite sex. An attractive member of the opposite sex. He'd stopped being 'invisible' to her. But shouldn't that have felt wrong? He was the closest thing she'd ever had to a brother; it should at the very least have felt weird.

Ryan waved his hand in front of her face. 'Hello, in there. Anybody home?'

'Huh?'

He smiled broadly at her expression. 'I don't think I've ever seen you so lost for words.' He stepped closer. 'You okay?'

Large green eyes blinked at him, as if putting him back into focus. Her heart beat erratically and she had to clear her throat before speaking. 'I think so.'

'Okay, I know I don't say this too often, but—' his smile softened affectionately '—you're right. This time, anyway.'

She raised an eyebrow. 'Oh, really?'

He nodded. 'Yeah. I'm attracted to you too.' Probably had been for half his damn life, he realised. But that information was a little too much for either of them to digest just yet. 'I've been thinking about it some and, to be honest, kissing a friend shouldn't feel like it feels when I kiss you. I wasn't prepared for that.'

'Neither was I.' She managed a small, shy smile. 'But you do kiss good, you know.'

Now it was Ryan's turn to blush. 'Yeah, well, there you go. I guess we all have to have a talent for something.'

'You're very cute when you blush too.' She couldn't resist teasing.

'And you know I hate it. Grown men aren't supposed to blush. Any more than they're supposed to have the thoughts about a "friend" that I've been thinking about you recently.'

'What kind of thoughts, exactly?'

Dangerous stuff. He knew it the moment he looked into her eyes and saw how dark they'd gone. Suddenly he was in grave danger of showing her exactly what his thoughts had been. Dark, hot thoughts that involved them doing things that no two platonic friends would ever think of doing. Made all the hotter, for some reason, by the very fact that they weren't 'allowed'. At least, not with Molly. But suddenly there was an opening for those fantasies, the tiniest flicker of a possibility that they might come true. He was twenty-one all over again.

'Grown-up thoughts, O'Brien. The kind that any man thinks about a woman when he finds her attractive.'

She focused her eyes on his broad chest, then back up into his eyes. Like a moth to an open flame, she stepped closer. 'And what exactly do these thoughts consist of?'

'Well, now that you've asked...' He stepped closer too, until their bodies almost touched. 'I guess they start with looking into your eyes to see if you're feeling any of this heat we've started up.' He did so.

Molly's throat went dry. 'And what do you see?'

The air crackled between them as he stared down into her eyes, as if by not touching they had increased the heat between them ten times. Ryan knew they were hitting the point of no return. From here there was no going back to the way they'd been before. Their relationship would change irrevocably.

'I see something that I've never seen there before.' His voice was seductively low. 'At least, not when you've looked at me.'

'What is it?'

The husky edge to her voice was almost his undoing. His body tightened spontaneously. 'I see desire. Moll, this thing has you just as hot as it has me, doesn't it?'

She stared up at him, her smile appearing slowly. 'Uh-huh.'

Lifting a hand from his side, he brushed her hair back from the side of her face with one long finger. He did it so, so slowly, barely allowing his warmth to touch her skin.

Her eyes flickered closed for a moment. 'I never knew.'

'Knew what?' His other hand moved to the small of her back, touched, and gently pulled her close until her curved body fitted snugly against him.

'That you could be so seductive.' She lifted her chin, opening her eyes to look into his, but instead found her gaze locked on his mouth. She swallowed hard, her throat now unbearably dry.

'Moll…' he leaned his head towards her '…you have absolutely no idea just how seductive I can be. Maybe it would just be easier if I showed you.'

Her eyes grew heavy as his breath fanned her face, warm and sweet. 'Yes,' she whispered. 'Maybe it would.'

Ryan smiled the slowest, sexiest smile she had ever seen. 'Those illicit thoughts of mine just didn't do justice to this, y'know.' His mouth touched hers.

The kiss was different this time. Almost as if by finally being honest with themselves, and each other, they were under no pressure to behave differently from how they felt. Molly wanted to be kissed by him, deeply and slowly. Ryan was only too happy to oblige.

He took his time, exploring the shape and texture of her lips as if he'd never kissed her before. She tasted sweet to him, felt so much softer than he could remember. Could this be Molly? Would she have responded to him like this if he'd kissed her years ago? His lips curved into a smile against her mouth. Did it really matter?

When the tip of her tongue brushed against his, Ryan felt his body harden, and was shocked by the force of his response. Only five minutes ago they'd been facing up to the fact that they were attracted to each other and now his libido was kicking in—with a vengeance. Too soon. It was too soon to be confronted with *wanting* her. What if he scared her? No. Even as his body cried out for a logical release his mind knew they had to take this slowly. It was all just too new, too fragile. They needed time. As a low moan grumbled in his throat he tore his mouth from hers. Breathing hard, he rested his forehead against hers. 'Wow.'

Fighting to regain her composure, she eventually smiled up at him. 'Wow, yourself. We're good at this bit, aren't we?'

'Too good.'

They stood in silence, arms around waists. Then Molly gently pulled away. 'About Kieran…'

Ryan stared at her. 'What do you want to do?'

'Well…' She took a breath. Turning away from him, she rested her hands on the porch rail and looked into the trees in the distance. She shivered, already missing the warmth from his body. In a few short minutes everything had changed beyond recognition. 'I don't know about you, but this is all a tad too new for me to be dealing with in front of his prying eyes. I'm not sure what Kieran might have to say on the subject—at least, not yet. Especially if he finds out how we started all this.'

'I'll not pretend I'm happy about hiding, O'Brien. But I'll agree, for now, because it's what you want. I don't want to argue with you about it.' The doubting voice re-emerged in his head.

She continued, still unable to look him in the face. 'It's just—I mean, we don't know where this is going ourselves. We could end up never able to face each other again.'

Ryan frowned, his voice stern. 'Okay, I get it. But, for the record, that'll never happen.'

'Callaghan.' She turned to face him, smiling sadly. 'We'll never be the same after this, and you have to know that as well as I do. It's one of the things that frightens me the most.'

'I'll always be here, just like I always have been.' He shook his head. 'I don't plan on going anywhere.'

Again she looked away. 'I hope you're right.'

There was silence.

She looked back again, at her 'rock', noted the sincerity in his eyes and smiled. 'Nothing's ever complicated to you, is it?'

Ryan managed a small laugh. 'Only round you.'

'We've started this now, so I guess we're going to see it through, one way or another. Let's not make it any more complicated by involving Kieran, okay?'

Unless he's already involved. It took a lot to keep the

frown from crossing his face. His first lie to Molly. Reaching out to take her hand, he squeezed her fingers in reassurance. 'Okay. But I won't hide in the shadows for ever—just remember that. We have nothing to be ashamed of.'

CHAPTER FIVE

Six years ago

SHE'D been living with Kieran for a year when the little voice started in the back of her head. At first she ignored it. Ignored the feeling in the pit of her stomach that said something wasn't right.

The first time she'd seen him she was seventeen and starting to change from an ugly ducking into—well, a duck, she supposed. He was the handsomest boy she had ever seen. And he was smart, funny, popular and rich. Inside a week she was besotted. But something in him seemed to die after university. There, he had been his happiest. Crowds of friends, sporting trophies and awards flooding in, and the never-ending round of parties to attend. Everyone on campus had just loved Kieran and being around him. Molly had been so proud of him, and so proud to be his.

But the outside reality of working life was something different. Now he had to work to maintain his wealth, and his sporting accolades were reduced to beating fellow board members in a weekly game of golf. And he had started to change into someone she didn't know so well any more.

She was twenty-three and she had been with him nearly six years. She should have been ready for marriage and that darned dozen kids. But then there was the voice.

'Are you drunk again, O'Brien?'

Molly glared up at Ryan. 'You make it sound like I'm an alcoholic. When's the last time you saw me rat-faced?'

He flumped down onto the large sofa beside her. 'Christmas.'

She snorted. 'See—damn near a year ago. So you can just go take a long walk off a short pier.'

They looked around the crowded room for a while. It was Molly's mother's fiftieth birthday and the house was packed to the seams. People she hadn't seen in years had spent all evening coming up and commenting on how much 'little Molly' had grown. And wasn't it just great now that she was a successful photographer? And wasn't it nearly time they bought a new hat for her wedding?

'So, how's life with you?'

'It sucks right now this very minute if you must know.'

Ryan studied her profile. 'How come?'

Molly took a long swallow of alcohol, continuing to study the crowd. 'Wish I knew, Callaghan.'

'Maybe I can help.'

She smiled at his gentle tone. 'Still trying to save the world, then?'

'Nope, handed over my cape on that one.'

'Sooo…' she turned large green eyes on him '…you're just going to rescue me instead?'

His dark eyes locked with hers for several long moments. She was troubled by something and had been for some time now. And he knew it. He just couldn't understand what it was. She should be happy as a pig in… Well, she had everything, didn't she?

'You need rescuing, Moll?'

Her smile was sarcastic. 'What? From my perfect life? Nah.'

'Isn't it perfect?'

For a split second she hated his calmness. Since he'd come back from his twenty-four-hour vocation of worrying the holy heck out of her he just seemed so goddamn calm.

Why was that? Not that she wasn't pleased about it. It was a lot easier sleeping at night when you knew your friend wasn't being macheted to death somewhere. But while she was so unsettled she just resented the heck out of his calm big self.

'What'd you do? Find the Holy Grail in the village we used to spend our holidays in?'

Ryan smiled slowly. 'Something like that.'

She glared at him. 'I swear, if you tell me you've found true love I'll throw up all over you.' The thought bothered her greatly.

She almost sighed as he reached out to tuck an errant strand of auburn hair behind her ear. She watched as he watched his finger, with soft, dark eyes, trailing it down her cheek and along her jaw.

'You're in a real bad twist, aren't you, my friend? So what is it?'

She stared at him. Then, unbidden, a tear rolled down her face. 'I don't know. I really don't know.'

Stunned by her own emotions she jumped up and ran from the room to the safety of her old bedroom. She wouldn't see Ryan or talk to him again until after she'd left for America.

Ryan didn't think he had ever been more frustrated in his life.

Kieran Rafferty was the one of the oldest friends he had—the only university friend he had kept over the years since those carefree days. They had survived the changes in their lives—just—and somehow adjusted to being friends now that they were adults. Ryan might not have liked everything about the new version of Kieran, but he'd accepted it. It just didn't alter the fact that right at that moment he could have quite happily not seen him for another six or seven months.

It wasn't that he wasn't enjoying having Kieran and his fiancée staying at his home. It wasn't that there wasn't laughter and banter echoing off the walls. And it certainly wasn't that the two 'couples' didn't greatly enjoy each other's company. It was just...

Well, if he was honest with himself it was just that having to *not* kiss Molly as often as he suddenly wanted to was completely messing up his head. Every time he looked at her, which seemed to be an awful lot recently, he found himself looking at her mouth and remembering. Remembering every time they'd kissed. Wanting more. It was hell. It was amazing. Who'd have thought it? Ryan Callaghan was seriously, *seriously* attracted to his best friend. And he couldn't even blame twenty-one-year-old hormones. Amazing. And frustrating.

'Ryan?'

He looked at Kieran as if he'd only just realised he was there. 'Sorry—what?'

Kieran grinned broadly, dimples appearing in his cheeks. 'You know, I don't think I've ever seen you so preoccupied. If I didn't know better, I'd have said you had it bad for some poor woman.'

'Me?' Ryan laughed loudly. 'Confirmed bachelor that I am? I don't think so, old pal.'

'Well, you look like I must have looked when I suddenly realised how Neave felt about me.'

'Nah!' He took a large swig of beer. 'Not me. I like my life the way it is. No hassles, no pressures. You've given all that up now, you know.'

Kieran leaned back against the porch rail and saluted his friend with his beer bottle. 'Wouldn't have it any other way. You don't know what you're missing.'

'Right.' A grin. 'That's why we're both stood down here waiting while those two spend for ever and a day getting ready to go to a simple dinner.'

'Well, knowing Molly and Neave as well as we do, believe me, if it's taking this long—' Kieran looked up at the second-floor windows '—the girls will be worth waiting for.'

On that note the 'girls' arrived.

Having taken a large mouthful of beer, Ryan almost choked to death. Molly was *not* playing fair. The length of her skirt bordered on the indecent. And there were those darned legs again!

'Wow!' Kieran said out loud what Ryan was thinking.

Instead he managed, 'You two scrub up pretty good.'

Molly raised an elegant eyebrow before reaching across to steal Ryan's beer. She took a sip before handing it back to him. 'Careful, now, Callaghan, you'll swell our heads. Any bit of wonder you've managed to stay single for so long. It's a miracle Maura can keep her hands off you!'

Kieran smiled at his fiancée but still managed to eavesdrop. He looked across at his friend. 'She's never still chasing after you?'

Ryan glared at Molly from hooded eyes. 'What can I say? I'm just irresistible to the opposite sex. Isn't that right, Moll?'

For a split second she looked astonished. Then she rose to the bait. 'Well, you know, it's been tough fighting off that attraction, but somehow the world still turns, the sun still rises and sets, the seasons still come and go...'

Kieran laughed. 'Yeah, we get the picture. God, imagine you two actually *fancying* each other. That'd be a laugh. Just be thankful you're not her type.'

Their taxi arrived. Ryan looked into Molly's eyes for a second before looking across at his friend. 'You're not kidding either.' A wink. 'I should know—I live with her, remember? How I managed to get through all those years without killing her stone dead stuns me.'

Kieran and Neave headed off the porch and down the long pathway to the waiting taxi. Ryan cupped Molly's elbow with one large hand as she walked down the steps, lowering his voice intimately. 'You *really* don't play fair, miss.'

She smiled, her eyes focused on the taxi and its newly acquired occupants. 'Really?'

'Are you deliberately trying to make me crazy?'

Noting that their audience seemed otherwise occupied, she turned to smile seductively at him. 'Now, knowing me as well as you do, do you honestly think I'd do any such thing on purpose?'

Ryan took a deep breath. 'Just so you understand that there'll be consequences.'

She laughed, glancing back towards the taxi. 'I have a feeling I'm going to quite enjoy this dinner.'

He let her walk ahead while he watched her swaying hips from behind. Frustration. It was a lonely word and she was going to have to pay.

A realisation—six years ago

'Who is she?'

'Who is who?'

Molly shook her head. The voice in her head had been getting louder for weeks now. 'You're seeing someone else, aren't you?'

Kieran looked at her across the dinner table, pale eyes thoughtful. Then he continued eating. 'I haven't the faintest idea what you're on about.'

'God, you must really think I'm stupid!'

'No.' He dabbed at the corner of his mouth with a napkin. 'What I think is that you're being ridiculous.'

Molly could feel tears welling up in her eyes. She swallowed hard to hold them off. 'No, what I am is hurt. Because she's not the first, is she?'

Kieran stared at her. 'What do you want me to say?'

'I want the truth! I think you owe me that.'

Thoughts seemed to flicker across his face in waves, then he crumpled. 'Molly, I'm so sorry.'

Molly's chest constricted. She'd known for some time that he was probably seeing someone else, but the 'others' had been a shot in the dark. God, was she so blind, so naïve, that she believed he was head over heels in love with her after all this time? How could she have thought that when for such a long time she'd been having doubts herself?

With supreme calmness she folded her napkin and stood up. 'I think I should go.'

He raised his eyebrows. 'You don't mean that. We can work this out, Molly. I know we can.'

Molly laughed wryly. 'If you say she meant nothing to you I swear I'll make you wear this bolognese.'

'I *love* you. You know that. We can get past this.'

She laughed at him again. 'You complete bastard. For months now I've been trying so hard to pretend that this would work. That any doubts I had were only natural at this stage of our relationship. And all that time you were sleeping with someone else. Well, you know what? She can have you.'

Kieran's chair toppled as he jumped up. 'Where are you going?'

She reached for the door handle. 'I'll let you know when I know.'

'Oh, I think we both know, don't we?' His face pushed

towards hers, his breath thick with wine and sarcasm. 'You'll go off to your *friend* Ryan, won't you? Just like always. Back to that incestuous little relationship you love so much. Maybe if you screwed him and got it over with then I wouldn't always feel like he's a spoke in our wheel.'

'Oh, no, you can't go blaming your insecurity about my relationship with Ryan for your inability to keep it in your trousers.' Molly's eyes were frosty. 'He's your friend, too, Kieran, or maybe you'd forgotten that.'

Kieran grimaced. 'For how long, when you tell him I've been playing around?'

'Let me go, Kieran, leave me alone.' Molly stared him in the eye. 'And I'll not tell him why we're splitting up. That way you'll only lose one friend in this.'

He looked momentarily shocked. 'Why would you do that?'

'Because he'd kill you if I told him.'

The game continued all the way through dinner at the local hotel. Innuendoes galore, frequent 'accidental' brushings of hands or feet or arms. To Ryan the room felt impossibly hot.

A band was playing in the adjoining room, and soon Kieran and Neave filtered through the double doors to dance.

'Hey, there.' Molly rested her chin on the palm of her hand, smiling slowly. 'How you doin', way over there?'

Ryan shook his head, laughing tensely as he turned to look across at her. 'You, my girl, are playing a *very* dangerous game here.'

Green eyes sparkled at him. 'Oh, really?'

'Yes, *really*.'

'How's that, then? Do explain.'

He leaned towards her, elbows resting on the table's

edge. 'You have been deliberately teasing me all evening and you know it.'

Lowering her long lashes, she watched her fingers toy with the stem of her wine glass. 'You think so?'

'You're old enough to realise that a game like this has consequences.'

Maybe it was the wine speaking, and maybe it was the frustration of playing friends while Kieran and his fiancée watched. Whatever the reason, it had been two whole days since Ryan had kissed her, and she wanted more. She was suffering from the lack of a decent night's sleep, thinking about kissing Ryan and being kissed by Ryan. Madness. So if she was suffering it seemed only reasonable that he suffer a little too....

'You've mentioned these consequences before.' Slowly she raised her eyes to look at him, her gaze focusing on his mouth. 'Maybe you should explain them to me in more detail.'

He groaned, running his fingers back through his dark hair. 'Do I know you? 'Cos you look very like a girl I used to know.'

'What was she like?'

'She was this *really* irritating kid to begin with.'

'What age?'

'Fourteen or fifteen—something like that. She used to tag along on all of my great adventures.'

'*Not* all of them. What age were you?' She smiled softly at the cherished memories.

'A very mature eighteen. Ready to take on the world.'

'Was she in the way, this kid?'

'No.' He smiled back at her. 'She was distracting and cheeky and entirely too smart for her own good.'

'She sounds nice. What happened to her?'

'She grew up and left us all behind.' He looked away.

'But she came back to her friends eventually, right?' Looking around to check it was safe, she reached across the table and touched her fingertips to his. 'So she's still here.'

Melted chocolate eyes looked back at her. 'No, she didn't. Someone different came back in her place.' He looked down at their hands, tangling his longer fingers with hers. 'Someone beautiful, wise and sexy as hell, who I'd never met before. Someone who has me more frustrated than I've ever been.' He moved his hand. 'Now, there's a confession.'

'I'm sorry, Ryan.'

Ryan noticed the use of his name again, how soft her voice had gone, and he ached. 'Are you?'

Molly looked surprised at the question. She opened her mouth to speak, and then stopped. Was she? Was she sorry that they'd changed their relationship?

'Come on then, you two.' Kieran and Neave appeared by the table. 'You both look like someone just died.'

Neave looked from one to the other and then reached her hand towards Ryan. 'Let's go shake ourselves to some music, Ryan. I believe you're quite the Patrick Swayze on the dance floor.'

Ryan laughed loudly. 'Somehow I don't think so, Neave. But I'm ready for some of that ''dirty dancing'' if you are.'

Kieran watched as his fiancée dragged a grinning Ryan away. He sat down in Ryan's place, turning to smile at Molly. 'You all right?'

She pulled her eyes away from the next room to look at the man who at one time had been the centre of her world. It felt like a lifetime ago. 'Sure. You look happy, Kieran, I'm pleased. She's a really nice girl.'

Kieran smiled the broad smile that had melted her heart

throughout her earlier years. 'Thanks. Ryan taking care of you for me?'

Her heart skipped a beat or two. Calm, Molly, stay calm. This was Ryan's friend. Ryan would hate himself if they hurt him intentionally. They both knew that, deep down. And she didn't want Ryan to feel guilty, or as if they had done anything at all wrong. It had to stay between them until they knew where they were going. It was the right thing to do. Molly knew that. Really she did. Really.

'The great protector? Oh, yeah, he's stopped me from being stolen away by marauders. I'm safe enough with him.' *As if…*

'I'm glad you decided to stay with him 'til your house is done. You're good company for each other.' Kieran reached across the table for his drink. 'Just like having a big brother around.'

Molly smiled at the out-dated description. If only Kieran knew. 'Well, in a kind of extremely irritating brother kind of a way, I guess,' she lied through her teeth.

Kieran smiled at the antics of Neave and Ryan on the dance floor, 'I love that big guy like a brother myself. He's the best friend I ever had.' Grey eyes looked into green. 'You *two* are the best friends I ever had. You both remind me of happier times in my life. Before I got old and discontented. You know, there's not a day goes by that I don't regret the mistakes I made in the past. I need you to know that. And that's said before I'm even drunk.'

'I know.'

'Here—' he leaned across the table towards her '—do you think we should try and find someone for him?'

There was a moment of stunned silence before Molly laughed tensely. 'For Callaghan?'

'Yeah. Well, you were on the money with me and Neave, so I reckon you should pick someone out for Ryan too.'

'Do you, now?' She took a large mouthful of her wine. 'And did you have someone in mind or shall I look her out myself?'

She tried hard to maintain a smile. If she could just try and stay calm then maybe she could keep on salvaging the memories she had of a better Kieran. A Kieran she had not only loved but actually *liked* a little. But he was Ryan's friend, and Ryan already believed that she had needlessly broken his heart. Ryan, being Ryan, cared for and protected his friends.

'What about Marie Donnelly? I heard he kissed her a few times. She's a nice girl.' He leaned closer, lowering his voice. 'He told me once he thought she was a looker. She's his type, you know. Stacked.'

Molly drank more wine, glaring at the dance floor. 'Did he say that? Well, then, it's a match made in heaven.'

'Uh-huh.' Kieran leaned back in his seat. 'I'll even make a bet on it.'

She leaned her head back and groaned. 'Believe me, my betting days are over.'

'Bet you they're not.'

'Kieran.' Her eyes narrowed. 'Believe me. I am *not* going to help you find a woman for Ryan. Not Marie Donnelly, nor anyone else for that matter, okay?'

The thought of Ryan with any another woman, let alone a woman that he'd already kissed in her absence, well...

'Aw, come on. Don't you want to see him as happy as I am?' He held his hand over his heart.

'See who happy?'

Molly's head snapped towards him so fast Ryan was convinced she must have broken her neck. 'O'Brien?' He pointed at Kieran. 'That guy giving you grief?'

She glared up at him. 'No, that's normally your job, isn't it?'

Kieran looked from one to the other and smiled. 'I was just making a little bet with Molly.'

'I see.' Ryan raised his eyebrows. 'Well, the forfeit must be hell, judging by your face.'

'Oh, I've heard some dumb dares of late, believe me.' Molly glanced away from Ryan. 'But this one's a peach.'

Ryan grinned at Kieran. 'Anything that's ticked her off this much has to be good. What did you dare her to do, my friend? It didn't have anything to do with beauty contests, did it?'

Kieran looked confused. 'No. Should it have?'

An elegant finger waved across the table. 'Don't go there.'

'Come on, now, you have to let me in on this.' Ryan laughed. 'What's the bet?'

Molly glared at him. 'You don't want to know.'

'Yeah, I do.'

'No, trust me. You don't.'

'Yeah, I do, O'Brien, honestly.'

Kieran was laughing loudly. 'Do you two ever get on?'

Molly stood up and faced off against Ryan. 'Okay, Callaghan, you asked for it. Your friend here just dared me to find you a woman.'

The smile froze on his face. 'You're kidding?'

She tilted her head to one side. 'Said you didn't want to know, didn't I?'

He felt like a stunned rabbit again. Car headlights all around him. Kieran laughed harder. 'Oh, boy, you should see your face!'

'He dared *you* to find me a woman.' Ryan chuckled slightly. 'That's very funny, Kieran.'

Molly smiled coolly at Kieran and then looked Ryan in the eye. 'He reckons you have quite an eye for a certain

Marie Donnelly. Said you thought she was a looker. Definitely your type.'

Ryan looked for the teasing light in her green eyes and was surprised by what he saw. Good God, she was actually jealous. Molly O'Brien was actually jealous of another woman because she thought he, Ryan Callaghan, might be attracted to that woman. He grinned widely.

She knew he knew. The minute he grinned she knew he knew she was jealous and she hated him for it. She hated him for the way he was making her feel a different emotion every day. But most of all she hated him for knowing her so well that he could see what she felt. Damn him.

Her eyes went cold and Ryan's grin faded. 'Now Molly…'

'Maybe I'll just take that bet.'

'Oh, no, you don't.' He frowned.

'No, really.' She winked at the others. 'That should liven things up a bit round here, don't you think?'

'Molly, I really don't need you to find me a woman.' His tone was flat, his face deadpan when she looked at him.

'You think?'

A frown. 'I know.' He dragged his eyes away from her, looking towards Kieran with a small smile. 'Call it off. *Now.*'

Molly smiled brightly at their audience. 'It's okay. I'd never find anyone who'd stick him for long enough.'

Without turning, Ryan glanced at her from the corner of his eye. 'There you go, then.'

Neave reached her hand out to touch Ryan's arm. She squeezed gently and smiled. 'Your time will come, Ryan. *I'll* even lay a bet on that.'

Molly smiled calmly, too calmly. 'Well, if she's got any sense at all she'll run and not stop running.'

CHAPTER SIX

America—six years ago

RYAN showed up in San Francisco five days after her arrival. There was such a loud banging on the door that Molly found herself reaching for a can of protective spray her roommate had given her. Then an all too familiar voice yelled out, 'O'Brien! O'Brien if you're in there you better open this door before I put it off its hinges!'

Molly froze in shock. It couldn't be.

'O'Brien, I mean it!'

With her breath held tight in her lungs, she yanked open the heavy door. The air then left her lungs in a sudden 'whoosh' as he pushed her back into the apartment. 'What the hell did you think you were playing at?'

'Well, goodness, Callaghan, it's lovely to see you too. Did you fly all the way over here just to bully me, or is this a social visit?'

He glowered at her from his advantageous height. 'A note! You left me a note! What am I to you? The equivalent of the milkman?'

Molly was shocked by his anger. She'd seen him angry before, witnessed him punching holes in walls after his parents were killed. But never before had his rage been directed at her. Not once.

'If I'd told you you'd have tried to stop me.'

'From running away from all the people that love you when you're this low? Now, why the hell would I do a stupid thing like that?'

Her voice was unnaturally calm. 'That's why I left the note.'

His anger seemed to dissipate in front of her eyes. Instead he stared at her, seeing right through to her very soul. With a heartfelt sigh he ran shaky fingers back through his hair, rumpling it ridiculously. Then he looked at her again. 'You scared everyone to death, y'know that?'

Still she was calm. 'I'm sorry.'

There were several moments of silence. And then, 'Are you okay?'

'You could've asked that over the phone—would have been cheaper.'

'I don't give a damn about the money. I was worried about you.'

Molly realised how tired he looked. Dark circles smudged his eyes, a beard was growing on his normally clean-shaven cheeks, his shoulders were slumped with fatigue. Had she done this to him? Had he chased clean across the planet just to check she was all right? With a twist of her heart, she realised she'd have done the same thing for him. It was just the way they were.

'I'm doing okay, Ryan.'

He raised a dark eyebrow at her. 'You call me Ryan again and I'll know you're not okay—okay?'

She smiled softly at him, not closing the distance between them any. 'I didn't want to worry you. I just needed to be not there any more. If that makes any sense at all.'

'Because of Kieran?'

She looked away, her eyes focusing on the rain sliding down the apartment windows. 'Partly.'

Ryan stepped towards her. 'And what else?'

As he got closer she stepped away from him. 'I needed to find out what I wanted to do with my life. And I knew I didn't want to be with Kieran.'

'You couldn't do that at home?'

She smiled a watery smile at the window. 'No.'

'Why not?'

'Because it's too complicated there. How can I decide what I want when I'm so surrounded by all the things that everyone else thinks matters the most? They don't see how I could possibly be missing anything from my life.'

'That's obviously a girl thing, 'cos you lost me on that.'

With a deep breath she turned to face him. 'I need time. I need time to find out who Molly O'Brien is and what she wants. All my life I've been Mum and Dad's little Molly, your Molly, and then Kieran's Molly. I don't know who I am.'

Dark eyes stared deep into the green he knew so well. 'Will you come home again?'

'Some day.'

'Promise me, O'Brien.'

'I promise.'

'Really?'

'Really.'

'Cross your heart and hope to die?'

She finally laughed. 'Keep this up and I'm never coming home.'

Molly couldn't sleep.

It wasn't any great surprise that she couldn't sleep because she hadn't had a good night's sleep for days now. Ever since... Well, ever since her life had gone and got complicated.

Damn him. How could he do this? How could her friend—her reliable, funny, caring, safety net of a friend—suddenly have caused her to turn into a frustrated, jealous, overly-emotional insomniac? It just wasn't fair. And it didn't make any sense at all.

She glanced over at the clock by her bed. Three-fifteen in the morning and she was no closer to sleep than she'd been when she'd made her excuses at twelve-thirty. It had become impossible to hold a smile and stay friendly when inside she wanted to beat Ryan to a pulp.

Houdini tested his claws out on her lap and she jumped from the window seat. 'Ow! You as well, Houdini? Well, the whole world's just queuing up to get me, isn't it?'

It wasn't that she was angry about Kieran's suggestion. No, it was more the fact that she'd felt so jealous at the very idea of Ryan with another woman. A woman that wasn't her. Doing the kinds of things she wanted to do so desperately that she couldn't sleep at night any more for thinking about it.

By four o'clock she could take no more. Moving as silently as she could around her room, she changed into jogging pants and a light sweater. A run would tire her out before dawn and then maybe she could have a lie-in. Sexual frustration was a bitch, she decided.

Ryan couldn't sleep.

He'd never needed that much sleep to begin with, but the sleep he needed he usually got. Until recently. He had to admit he was beginning to miss sleeping. Well, the kind of sleeping where a person closed his eyes and didn't think or feel anything until he woke up again had been nice. He could remember those nights if he concentrated really hard.

Women! Good grief, to think Kieran actually thought he needed *another* one to cause problems in his ordered little part of the universe. One was plenty to deal with.

He was in trouble with Molly *again*. It wasn't even his fault this time and yet he was in trouble. It wasn't *his* fault she'd had an attack of the green-eyed monster. A smile crossed his lips at the thought that would have at one time amused him above anything else. Then he frowned again. Really, it wasn't as if he'd done anything wrong at all. Nope, he was completely and utterly innocent. This time.

The digital read-out on his alarm read three-thirty. Punching his pillow, he rolled over. She needn't think he was going to try and apologise or anything. He hadn't done *anything* wrong. Kieran's dumb dare had been his doing, not Ryan's. And it wasn't his damned fault she'd got jealous.

Three-forty. He threw the covers back and sat up. So maybe at one time he had thought Marie was attractive. He hadn't been with anyone at the time. Could he even say he was 'with' anyone now? What was he? Confused. Yeah, that was it, confused. And frustrated. Very, very frustrated. He wanted to kiss Molly again so badly it was a physical ache. And as to where the rest of his nocturnal thoughts headed, well… Damn her.

Turning on a lamp, he began to pace, his bare feet padding softly on the warm wooden floor. Maybe if she'd never come home he could have continued to lead his life in the same calm, orderly fashion he'd found he liked. Not that he wanted never to have known her at all. He wouldn't trade his years of being around Molly for the world. When he'd lost his parents to the accident she had become his only family.

He glanced at the clock again at four. To think that the scrawny, freckly teenage girl he'd teased mercilessly had got her revenge by changing into some maddening sexy female. A female who tugged at his fragile libido every time she glanced up at him with those warm eyes. It wasn't right. Damn her.

Well, she needn't think he owed her *any* kind of an apology. She had spent the entire evening flirting with him and teasing until he'd wanted to kiss her senseless and much more. Nope, he wasn't going to apologise. No way.

He went downstairs to make coffee at four-thirty.

She was standing with her arms outstretched, leaning against the doorframe as she tried to catch her breath. With her head bowed she didn't hear him come into the kitchen.

With only the dim light from the porch behind her she was silhouetted by a soft glow that set her hair on fire. Ryan watched the rise and fall of her breasts. Heard the gasping of her breath in the still night air. Saw the glisten of moisture on her skin. It was almost an extension of his hot and heavy night-time dreams. What was real? What was fantasy? He couldn't seem to tell any more. He swallowed hard. His body hardened. Dear Lord, how was he supposed to fight against someone who embodied all of his fantasies?

Still breathing hard, she looked up and saw him. Her breath caught.

'I'm sorry.'

Turning to face him, she placed her hands on her hips and raised her chin. 'What for? Making my life difficult?'

A smile. 'Well, yeah, there's that. And then there's Kieran's dumb suggestion.'

She bowed her head for a moment. 'That wasn't your fault. You don't need to apologise for that. I overreacted.'

Okay. That had worked. He took a step closer, looking around the room. 'I, uh, was going to make coffee. You want some?'

He felt the raw tension between them, tingling in the air. It had never been there before—at least not that he could remember. And he wasn't quite sure he liked it much.

She laughed. 'No, thanks. The last thing I need is something else to help me *not* sleep.'

'Right.' He moved forwards again. 'I know how that goes.'

'I thought a run might tire me out some.' She watched him with guarded eyes as he walked across the kitchen. 'Another Americanism, I guess.'

'Yeah.' His eyes were fixed on hers. 'Insomnia is a terrible thing.'

'Callaghan, stop.'

He stopped and stared at her.

'I can't do this any more.' She held her arms out in surrender. 'I can't keep tiptoeing around you like this while the rest of the time I'm so darned frustrated. This is awful— I mean *really* awful. I don't think I've ever felt worse in my entire life.'

'I know.'

'And the thing is, if I felt like this with anyone else then I'd walk away, or—well, I guess I'd do something about it. But I just can't seem to decide what to do any more.'

'Me either.'

'I'm absolutely terrified.'

Ryan nodded. 'Me too.'

'If this doesn't work, and we have to start all over, we'll never be the same and I don't want to lose my friend.'

'You won't.' He stepped closer.

Her voice caught. 'You can't guarantee that. And yet, even though I tell myself that nothing is worth losing my friend over, I can't stop wanting you.'

'Ditto.'

Molly shook her head, staring up into his dark eyes. Then, taking a deep, shaky breath, she threw herself forward and kissed him.

It was a frantic, hungry meeting of mouths. All the frustration built up inside them was spilling out into a desperate joining of lips and tongues. This time there were no reservations, hesitations or doubts. Molly stood on her toes and pushed her body as close to him as she could manage with the layer of clothing between them.

A groan rumbled low in his throat as he enclosed her small waist with his arms. His mouth moved desperately over hers. This was what he'd spent sleepless nights thinking about. This was the only thing that made sense any more. He'd done nothing but think about how it felt to kiss her and now she was here, in his arms. Her body tight against him and yet not tight enough. She moved her hips across his and his lower body responded immediately.

Molly felt it, and she smiled against his lips. It was the first time in a very long time that she'd felt in control. She moved her hips against him again and he rewarded her with another low groan. He wanted her as much as she wanted him.

Moving her hands from behind his neck, she wriggled to get her arms underneath his, so that she could touch him without having to separate their mouths. Her fingers found the bottom of his T-shirt and pushed it upwards so that she could lay her palms flat against the taut skin on his stomach. As she moved her thumbs along the band of his shorts he tensed. Dragging his mouth from hers, he looked down at her flushed face.

'Molly—' He lifted his hands, brushing the backs of his fingers along her cheeks. 'Slow down. This doesn't need to happen in a hurry.'

Her eyes flickered open and she smiled slowly. 'Doesn't it? You speak for yourself.'

Ryan laughed softly. 'All these years and I never once dreamed we'd be doing this. You're making me absolutely crazy—you know that, right? I've never wanted anyone this much in my entire life.'

'Callaghan, I hope so. 'Cos then we'll be about even.' She spread her fingers wide on his abdomen. 'This is the first thing that has felt completely right to me in a long time.'

His breathing quickened. 'We can't do this while Kieran and Neave are here.' It was almost a question. Then he smiled a lazy, sexual smile, his voice a husky whisper. 'They might hear.'

'I know.' She moved her thumbs down again. 'But that doesn't mean we can't practise a little.'

The desperate need inside him invited the paranoid voice in his head to be slightly curious as to why it should matter whether they made love while Kieran was in the house. But then, it had been him that made the statement. All his body knew was how much he wanted her. It couldn't give a damn about Kieran's feelings on the matter.

Leaning down, he touched his mouth to hers again for a long, slow kiss. Then he raised his head an inch. 'I guess I could make a pact with you to be quiet?'

Molly smiled at the teasing tone in his voice and the sparkle in his dark eyes. 'Callaghan, somehow I don't think it'll be you making the noise.'

He took a deep breath. Then, as he touched his forehead to hers, he moved his fingertips softly across her back.

She gasped. 'And I'm not kidding about that.'

'I want you to make a *lot* of noise,' he whispered.

Her heart raced. *'Ryan—'*

'Which is why we're going to wait until we have an empty house and all the time in the world.'

Despite how much her body ached, she knew he was right. 'You do realise if we wait much longer we're going to be so frustrated that it's only going to take us about five minutes.'

Ryan lifted his head and smiled a slow, sensuous smile. 'It's going to take *way* more than five minutes. I'll make quite sure of that, O'Brien. Trust me.'

* * *

NO POSTAGE
NECESSARY
IF MAILED
IN THE
UNITED STATES

BUSINESS REPLY MAIL

FIRST-CLASS MAIL   PERMIT NO. 717-003   BUFFALO, NY

POSTAGE WILL BE PAID BY ADDRESSEE

HARLEQUIN READER SERVICE
3010 WALDEN AVE
PO BOX 1867
BUFFALO NY 14240-9952

Do You Have the LUCKY KEY?

PLAY THE Lucky Key Game

and you can get

FREE BOOKS and a FREE GIFT!

Scratch the gold areas with a coin. Then check below to see the books and gift you can get!

YES! I have scratched off the gold areas. Please send me the **2 FREE BOOKS** and **GIFT** for which I qualify. I understand I am under no obligation to purchase any books, as explained on the back of this card.

386 HDL D39Y   **186 HDL D4AG**

FIRST NAME   LAST NAME

ADDRESS

APT.#   CITY

STATE/PROV.   ZIP/POSTAL CODE

2 free books plus a free gift   1 free book

2 free books   Try Again!

Offer limited to one per household and not valid to current Harlequin Romance® subscribers. All orders subject to approval. Credit or Debit balances in a customer's account(s) may be offset by any other outstanding balance owed by or to the customer.

Molly still cared about Kieran's feelings, for some unknown reason. Despite everything. But she had never wanted him to leave more in her entire life. It was just that it felt as if he was in the way. And if it weren't for a deepseated need to save Ryan any pain she would have told him to get lost by now. But she still felt that in hurting Kieran's feelings she'd be hurting Ryan by default. And she just couldn't do that.

For the last few days she and Ryan had been sneaking around like two hormonal teenagers, and she just couldn't seem to stop grinning. It was only a matter of time before Kieran would open his eyes for a moment or two and notice what was happening right beneath his nose. And then what would they say? *Sorry, Kieran, but until we spend a couple of weeks in the bedroom we really can't decide whether or not this is just lust, so we decided to keep it quiet.*

But, still, she had to admit lust was certainly involved in the whole thing in a big, big way. The Molly she had been a few weeks ago would have been completely amazed at the effortless manner in which Ryan could send her body into waves of longing and frustration. The new Molly simply wanted more. And soon.

Maybe she should have been spending time considering the repercussions of making love with her best friend, but all she knew was that she wanted him. She'd never experienced that depth of longing before and it was, simply, amazing.

She thought about the twenty minutes they'd spent in his office that lunchtime and smiled broadly. It was like being two kids discovering foreplay for the first time. Touching and tasting felt *so* good. Fumbling with clothing to get closer to skin was the most thrilling of games and—well, it was just as well his door had a lock.

Kate watched her for half an hour and then could take

no more. 'You're like the cat that got the cream. You've gone and done it with him, haven't you?'

'Kate!'

Her friend placed her hands on her hips, one eyebrow rising. 'I'm not stupid, Molly. I've seen that look before—even worn it a few times. You have the look of a woman who has been well and truly satisfied.'

Molly looked affronted. 'I have been no such thing.'

'Oh, yes, you have.'

'Kate, I have not.' She stared her straight in the eye. 'Really.'

Kate considered her carefully. Molly looked away, busying herself with paperwork.

'Then why smile so much all the time?'

Molly grinned. 'Life, I guess.'

'Right. That'll do it every time.'

They were silenced by the appearance of customers who kept them busy for an hour. Then, 'So can I assume things are going well with you and Ryan?'

'You just don't quit, do you?' Molly sighed.

'I'm your friend; I care about what's going on in your life. I just like to know what's happening, that's all.'

She looked so hurt that Molly couldn't lie to her. 'Things are going very well, thank you.' She grinned again.

Kate positively glowed. 'I knew it!'

'But don't you go planning the rest of our lives for us. We don't have a clue where this is going yet.'

'But you are together, right?'

Molly looked around the shop before lowering her voice. 'Yes.'

Kate looked around the shop too, lowering her voice to match Molly's. 'Is it a big secret, then?'

She screwed her nose up slightly. 'Uh, well, it's…complicated.'

Two eyebrows raised at her. 'In what way complicated? Ryan's got a secret wife hidden away like Mr Rochester?'

Molly tilted her head, sighing. 'Hardly.'

'I think you should know this kind of suspense could well put me into early labour.'

Green eyes scanned the shop again, as did blue. 'Well, it's like this…' She cleared her throat. 'Kieran kind of doesn't know.'

Kate stared at her. Molly waited patiently for a moment and then demanded, 'What, Kate?'

'We're whispering like schoolkids because you're too scared to tell your ex you're sleeping with his friend?'

Molly frowned hard. 'I am *not* sleeping with Ryan.'

'Yet.'

'And, anyway, when you put it like that it sounds dumb. It's not that simple.'

Kate sighed dramatically. 'Then try explaining it to me.'

Molly glanced around the shop again. Then, with her back to the counter, she looked at Kate. 'I would just prefer it if he didn't know yet, that's all. I mean, who's to say that we'll still be together in another few weeks? This could all be a storm in a teacup! It'll be tough enough just staying friends without half the world on our case about it.'

Keeping one eye on the shop door, Kate studied her face. 'What makes you so sure that you two won't work?'

'In the happily-ever-after sense?'

'Yeah.'

A sigh. 'Kate, why now? Why, when we've known each other all this time, is this only happening *now*?'

Kate shrugged. 'Maybe it's just the right time. Maybe you two weren't ready for this until now.'

'You mean fate?'

'Something like that.'

She shook her head. 'I started out like everyone else,

believing in that "meant for each other" crap. But I've *been* in love, Kate—and, trust me, not everyone gets the roses-round-the-door ending that you got. You were very lucky.'

Another group of customers entered the shop, taking their time to look through the souvenirs and allowing Molly a little thinking space. She had never been in a relationship this complicated before. The few that she had been in had been simple, clear-cut and, in the end, failures. Her one very serious relationship had been easy from the beginning. She had been instantly attracted to Kieran and he had been attracted to her, if a little slower to notice. It had worked—almost. Except for the little voice in her head, unforeseen changes to her partner's personality, and a slight case or two of needless philandering. But it had never been the rollercoaster ride she was experiencing now.

'You're a cynic. I can't believe I never knew that about you.' Kate studied her as the last customer left. 'Ryan cares more about you than any other female I've ever known of. Surely that means something?'

'And I care about him too, Kate. That's just the thing—don't you see? It never once occurred to me that I'd be this attracted to him—well, you know.' She blushed. *'Physically.'*

Kate looked surprised. 'Never?'

'Never. At least, I don't think so.'

'You're kidding?'

Molly laughed wryly. 'Just because you fancied the pants off him when we were teenagers doesn't mean I felt the same way.'

'Why on earth not?'

'Aw, come on, Kate.' She moved away to tidy some of the displays their latest customers had been looking through. 'I never looked at him like that. He was just...*there*. And then there was the Kieran thing.'

'Hmm.' Kate pursed her lips. 'Well, we both know what I thought of that at the time. I could never get why you liked him more.' She sighed. 'I guess we never want what's best for us when we're teens, do we?'

Molly swung round to look at her. 'What does that mean? Kieran *was* best for me back then. Things just didn't work out, that's all. I couldn't have had Ryan even if I'd wanted him then. Regardless of the fact that he wouldn't have wanted *me* that way.'

'I don't think either you *or* Ryan would have been ready for a serious relationship then—but, Molly, no one could ever quite figure out what it was with you and Kieran. In the beginning you mooned after him like he was God's gift. And when he didn't notice at first you just chased all the harder. Then what happened, huh?'

'Chased?' Her curiosity was sparked. 'You think I chased after him? Doesn't that make me sound a touch desperate? I was *in love* with Kieran, for goodness' sake. I couldn't see straight. I thought he was gorgeous. Ryan was just—well, just an irritating elder brother who cared about me. That's all.'

'Well, if you say so.' Kate shook her head. 'But if you thought of him in a brotherly way then you wouldn't be where you are right now. You didn't look at him back then 'cos he was right in front of your nose the whole time. There was no chasing involved, no mystery, no challenge. And maybe if you'd noticed him physically back then you wouldn't have been ready. I mean, think about it—would you have been up for this when you were eighteen? Were things ever this intense with you and Kieran? With Ryan there was never any question of your love for him. In the end, with Kieran, there was. You should just think about that for a moment, my girl.'

Molly stared at Kate with wide eyes. Wheels turned in her mind. What if Kate was right? No, no, that would mean throwing away an anchor that she'd had for a long, long time. Ryan was the one constant in her life. She'd never thought of him in any other way, had she? When she'd been down, one phone call to him had picked her back up again. Ryan was her safety net, her voice of reason. At times he'd even been her conscience. She needed him. It was a fact she'd always accepted. To have to analyse those feelings was to risk a lifetime of memories. She'd have to recategorise them completely, look at their relationship in a new light. Could she have been *that* blind?

And as for the intense nature of the physical compatibility they seemed to have—could she have dealt with it at eighteen? With a twist of her heart she realised it would probably have frightened her to death. She hadn't really known what she wanted at eighteen. Well, no, that wasn't entirely true either. She'd *thought* she'd wanted Kieran. And look where that had got her....

'Hey.' Kate's hand squeezed Molly's forearm. 'You okay?'

Molly blinked at her and then smiled weakly. 'This isn't helping any, you know.'

'Oh, Lord, I'm sorry. I don't mean any harm by what I say.'

'I know.' She patted her friend's hand. 'I know that. It's just that my relationship with Ryan has always been—well, rock-solid, I guess. And right now we're on a shaky section of ground. Nothing looks the same any more.'

'That must be quite scary.'

'It is. But the truth is I can't stop it. I just have to wait and see where it's going.'

Kate nodded. 'And you'd rather it wasn't made any more difficult by Kieran getting involved too, right?'

'He'll try to be the voice of doubt. He'll see all the pitfalls. And with the way I feel right now—well, I don't think I can hear it from him. *And* it might hurt him to see us together like that, even after all this time.' She glanced downwards. 'Ryan would feel guilty about that.'

'I understand.'

Kate noticed movement outside the shop's large windows. Ryan was walking through the main coach park with a small group of tourists, pointing out the park's amenities. His smile was broad, and even from a distance she was sure his eyes were shining. 'Well, whatever it is that's happening with you two, it's certainly put as broad a smile on his face as it's been putting on yours.'

Molly looked out and smiled. 'Yeah, I guess it has at that.'

Kate shook her head, laughing. 'Oh, boy, you've really got it bad, haven't you? I'd lay odds on you two making it.'

'Never, *ever* bet on anything, Kate. Especially love. Trust me.'

'Cynic.'

'Realist.'

'Whatever fits.'

'O'Brien, has anyone ever told you what a cynic you are?'

Molly raised her chin an inch to look down her nose at him. 'I, Callaghan, am a realist.'

Ryan laughed. 'Is that so?'

'I analyse things carefully, calculate the odds, then approach the matter *realistically*.' She blinked slowly to emphasise the point, then stuck out her tongue. 'So there!'

He laughed harder, his chest vibrating beneath her hand.

With Kieran and Neave absent from the house they had been making the most of their momentary freedom. Watching a video together wasn't anything new. But trying to watch a video while lying across the couch, her head on his chest, her body close to his and all their newfound sexual awareness surrounding them was definitely a new experience.

In order to try and take her mind off his wandering fingertips she had spent the last ten minutes explaining her theory as to why the two leading characters in this disaster movie weren't going to make it to the end without another momentous cliff-hanger. And so the debate had begun...

'Seriously, though, why shouldn't they make it through to the end and live happily ever after?'

Molly raised her head. 'Life will inevitably conspire to get them.' She smiled. 'If not, then the scriptwriters sure as heck will.'

'Like I said, you're a cynic.'

'We are what we are. I just prefer to call it realism.' She set her head down against his chest again and wriggled in closer to his side, one leg sprawling over his. 'Lying on you is comfier than lying on this old sofa, y'know. You kept that a secret.'

'Ah, now.' One hand ran down along her back, sending tingles up her spine. 'That's another of those things you didn't know about me.'

She lifted her head to look down into his eyes. 'Oh is that so?'

Ryan stretched upwards to kiss the end of her nose. 'Well, you didn't know I was a good kisser, did you?'

'And will for ever more never be allowed to forget I said so.'

'True.'

Green eyes rolled heavenwards even as she chuckled.

'So, you reckon I don't know you—that's what you're saying here?'

He nodded, moving his hand under the edge of her short blouse to touch the soft skin on her back. It was rapidly becoming a familiar drug, his touching her. 'Oh, you *know* me, all right, but there are things *about* me you don't know—just like there are things about you *I* don't know. And I am thoroughly enjoying discovering.'

Her pulse quickened as his fingertips made small, light circles on her skin. Within a very short space of time she'd got used to the thrill his touch sent through her nerve endings. Her body knew where those small touches would eventually lead, and it wanted those next steps—soon.

'Like what kind of things, exactly?'

'Well...' his eyes darkened '...knowing a person as a friend is a bit different to knowing them as a lover, don't you think?'

'Yes.' Her voice became husky. 'Much different.'

A smile—a slow, lazy, impossibly sexy smile. 'You see, it would never have occurred to me that your skin was *this* soft.'

'I see.' She wriggled closer, placing a light kiss on the edge of his mouth. 'Go on.'

'Or that your hair smelt this good close up.'

Another light kiss. 'That shampoo was worth every penny.'

'Or that you tasted so good.' He rolled over until she was pinned between his body and the back of the couch. 'So good that I'd want to kiss you in places that no friend would ever—'

'Shut up Callaghan.' She pulled his head towards hers, her fingers tangling in the slight coarseness of his dark hair. If kissing had been an Olympic sport then Molly was quite sure they'd be up for a gold medal. When he kissed her she could think of nothing else.

Warmth spread across her body as his tongue danced with hers. Never before had she been this ready to make love with someone. It was as if the moment he touched her he lit a touch paper inside her body. If he could do that just by kissing her and running his hands over her body, then what would he do to her when they actually made love?

Molly moaned deep in her throat. The frustration of their long sessions of heavy foreplay was beginning to take its toll on her.

Ryan knew he couldn't keep doing this without a logical conclusion. The thought of making love with Molly was one that never completely left his mind at any point of the day or night. It was like being twenty-one all over again. His hand shook as he touched her, moving from the skin at her back to set his palm flat against her stomach. With one slightly rough fingertip he lightly touched the skin at the waistband of her sweatpants. He felt her gasp air from his mouth and his body hardened.

'Do you have any idea how much I want you?' He wrenched his mouth from hers to ask the question.

She didn't answer. Instead, her tongue moistened her lips ever so slowly, and then she smiled, looking up at him from hooded eyes.

Ryan groaned. 'If Kieran doesn't go home soon, I swear I'll suffocate him while he sleeps.'

'That's not very nice.' She smiled seductively before kissing him again. As she nipped playfully against his bottom lip she felt another groan deep in his chest. It was just too difficult to keep fighting the wanting. Her need was too great now.

With amazing dexterity Ryan managed to open the buttons on the front of her blouse one-handed. His lips formed a smile against hers as he discovered lace. 'If I'd known all this time that you wore this kind of stuff under your clothes I think I'd probably never have kept my hands off you.'

Long fingers brushed against her heated skin at the edge of the lace. 'How long did they say they'd be out?'

Floods of warmth radiated low in her body. She gasped, her head arching back as his fingers continued their gentle exploration.

'How long?'

When she looked into his eyes she was lost. His pupils were so large his eyes were nearly black. She reached one small shaking hand towards his cheek, running her thumb across the slight coarseness she found there.

Her voice was a husky whisper. 'Long enough...'

CHAPTER SEVEN

RYAN carried her upstairs, his mouth never leaving hers. Still kissing her, he carried her to her room, setting her reverently on the bed.

'I'm in Molly O'Brien's bedroom.'

He grinned a lop-sided grin as he joined her on the patchwork comforter. 'I haven't been in your bedroom in years.'

Molly laughed, her eyes glittering as he started to undress her. 'Mmm, not since college anyway.'

He leaned his head to the curve of her neck. 'I seem to recall you had this nightshirt with a bear on the front. It was sexy as hell.'

Molly tried to concentrate on his words as his tongue touched her skin, tasting the salt on its surface. As she twisted on the bed he placed his arm across her ribcage, keeping her still.

'God, you thought that was sexy?'

His voice was muffled. 'You made loads of stuff look sexy.'

His mouth continued moving over her skin in damp circles. She moaned and he smiled against her skin, moving his mouth further up the side of her neck.

'Way back then you thought I was sexy?'

His breath tickled against her ear, his voice whispering. 'You, O'Brien, have no idea what you did to my libido in my early twenties. It's just not something you tell a friend in idle conversation.'

Her mind flickered back to her earlier conversation with Kate. She smiled, then, winding her fingers through his hair, pulled his head back so that she could see his eyes. 'Oh, is that right? And now?'

A smile. 'Now I'm telling you as your *lover*. You are probably the sexiest woman I have ever known. And I want you.'

The words empowered her, giving her new-found strength in what she was capable of doing to him. The kiss was hot, her mouth open and wet against his as her fingers moved restlessly through his hair, then down across his shoulders. Touching the material of his T-shirt, she moaned against his mouth, 'Off.'

Her order was immediately obeyed. He pulled the shirt over his head and then he was back, his mouth on hers, hot skin against her skin. Her skin so very soft, *everywhere*. Lord, but he'd just known it would be.

'I love how you feel.'

The words tickled against her swollen lips as he dragged one long finger lightly along the base of her ribcage. As a low giggle erupted from her mouth he smiled again, the tip of his nose resting against hers.

'And how ticklish you are. You always were very ticklish.'

She squirmed beneath him, laughing louder as he repeated the motion. 'Stop! You rat, that's not fair.'

Dark eyes sparkled in the dim light of the room. 'There you go with the name-calling again. You need to learn my given name, you know.'

He dragged the same tickling finger further down her side, then ran it across her waistband. 'Let's see now—what was my name?'

The butterfly lightness of his touch drew another gasp from her lips. 'Callaghan—'

'Nope, that's not it.' Another searing hot kiss. 'Don't you

think that now we're this *close* you should at least call me Ryan?'

She tried to answer but was distracted by the dipping of his dark head towards her ear. His teeth nipped at her earlobe, gently tugging.

'Oh, my God.'

His head raised and he smiled at her. 'No, just Ryan will do.'

Molly smiled, reaching out to run her finger along the fullness of his lower lip. She'd never before noticed how sexy his lower lip was, with its sensual pout. But, having experienced the full wealth of his lips' talents, she was more able to fully appreciate it now.

His eyes sparkled warmly at her as he hooked a thumb under her waistband. 'Now, what was it you said earlier? Oh, yeah, I remember. *Off.* That was it.'

'Yessir.' She saluted, then raised her hips slightly, allowing him to remove the offending article.

Another kiss. 'I would very nearly settle for sir you know.'

Molly kissed him back, silencing him for several moments and eliciting a renewed hardening of his body against her. She smiled slowly at him, her voice seductive. 'In your dreams.'

'You've no idea what's been in my dreams.' He touched his nose against hers and stared into her eyes, close up. 'But then this is even better than I'd imagined.'

Molly arched her hips as his fingers touched once, twice, then slid beneath her body to draw her closer to him. 'Ryan, please—'

Kissing her deeply, he let his tongue mimic the motion her body craved so badly. Then with a shrug he was out of the rest of his clothes. When he spoke his voice was husky with need. 'Say it again.'

Moving her hands to draw him closer, she looked up into his dark eyes. 'Please, Ryan. I can't wait any more.'

Molly's senses were tuned to the sound of their harsh breathing in the silent house, the weight of his body on hers. And then the world went silent.

Eventually Ryan lifted his head from her neck to look down into her face. 'Hey, there, how you doin'?'

Her mouth slowly turned upwards at the edges at the sound of his low voice. 'Forgotten my name already, Callaghan?'

Long lashes slowly fanned upwards as she looked at his flushed face. As if checking her face for signs of doubt, he explored her every feature before a familiar teasing light twinkled in his dark eyes. 'Sorry, do I know you?'

A car door closed outside the house; the sound of voices drifted through to them. Molly's eyes widened. 'They're back! You've got to go.'

'Maybe I don't want to.' He frowned down at her.

But Molly was already squirming away from him. 'They can't find us like this. Don't be ridiculous. We agreed, remember?'

Ryan rolled onto the edge of the bed and reached for his clothes, his movements much slower than Molly's.

Pulling on a nightshirt and dressing gown with quick motions, she glanced across the room at him. 'Please?'

Without fastening his jeans, he grabbed his T-shirt, then turned to look at her, his face dark in the light from the hallway. 'We haven't done anything wrong here, so just remind me again why it is we're sneaking around like two teenagers? 'Cos I *really* need to know.'

'Not now.' She placed the palms of her hands against his chest, pushing him into the hallway as the front door closed. 'We can talk about this tomorrow.'

He dug his heels in, stopping at her doorway. 'Why not now?'

After a nervous glance towards the stairs Molly allowed herself to look into his face, and was surprised by the look she saw there. Did he feel she was rejecting him in some way? How could he possibly think that after what had just happened between them? She blinked at him in confusion. He had agreed with her about not telling Kieran, so what was wrong?

Her voice was low. 'Do you always go parading around in front of your friends when you've just had sex with someone?'

The reasoning made him angry. 'Like hell I do. It's no one else's business. But this is different and you know it.'

'How is it? You want to wait here 'til they catch us at it? Or would you prefer we walk round the house naked until they figure it out?'

'Well, no, but—'

She glared at him. 'They didn't call us up to tell us the moment they slept together, Callaghan, so why the hell should we be telling them?'

Ryan realised she was making him sound ridiculous, but still a part of him wanted to shout to the world that...

What? He'd just slept with Molly O'Brien? No, that wasn't enough. That he'd just had the most fulfilling sex of his life with his best friend? That made him sound like a complete heel. And it wasn't enough either. So what was it, then?

While Molly glanced towards the stairway again he looked at her. Her hair still mussed from their oh-so-recent lovemaking, her cheeks flushed. His chest tightened at the sight of her, his body stiffening with recent memories. She was just so damned gorgeous. With the force of a kick in the chest he realised the truth. He was in love with her. Good God, he always had been, hadn't he?

When she looked back at him her eyes were pleading. 'Please, if we have to ruin what happened with a row, can't we do it tomorrow?'

Both heads turned at the familiar creak of the first stair. Ryan looked back at her, his voice low. 'Nothing could ruin what just happened.'

'God, I know.' She smiled softly. 'We *will* tell them, Ryan. The two of us, *together*. Just not right now, okay?'

For a split-second he hesitated, his newfound discovery almost on his lips. Then, 'Okay.'

Molly barely had a second to see his door close before she closed her own and footsteps passed outside her room.

Four years earlier

'He's still not over you, you know.'

Molly sighed at Ryan's words. It had been two years since she'd left Ireland and Kieran behind. 'How can he not be?'

'Well, maybe the man loved you more than you loved him. Had that thought ever occurred to you?'

She changed the phone to her other ear before answering. 'I *did* love him. I just didn't love him enough, is all.'

There was faint crackling on the line as Ryan thought. 'How do you know, do you think?'

'Know what?'

'Whether or not you love someone enough.'

Molly popped another potato chip into her mouth. 'You just do. I guess it'll feel like you've loved them for ever.'

'Hell, you don't still read those romance things, do you?'

A giggle. 'Don't have time to. Anyway, just because I'm crap at relationships doesn't mean I don't believe in love.'

She could almost see his smile.

'Who says you're crap at relationships? You still have me.'

'You're easy.'

'As if you'd know.' His laughter was a low rumble down the line. 'Anyway, how's this new man of yours?'

'Brad.'

'What?'

She smiled again. 'His name's Brad.'

'It would be, wouldn't it?'

'For your information he's a really nice guy.'

'But not "the one", eh?' It was a statement more than a question. 'So, are you still looking for Mr Right or do you think maybe you might already have left him behind in Ireland?'

Molly sighed. 'Look, I know he's your friend, and believe me I'm sorry he's hurt but it just wasn't right. I knew I couldn't spend for ever with him. And even if I don't find that rightness with someone else, it doesn't mean I don't still think I deserve it.'

'I hope you do find it, O'Brien.'

They stayed in companionable long-distance silence for a moment, and then Molly asked, 'What about you?'

'What about me?'

'You believe in love?'

'Dunno.' He swallowed a mouthful of coffee. 'I guess so.'

'You know sometimes you can just be such a *man*.'

'Now, how come you manage to make that sound like an insult?'

Molly smiled affectionately, knowing he couldn't see

her. 'You wait—the right woman will steal your heart away before your very eyes.'

'And we'll live happily ever after in a kingdom far, far away. Yeah.' He grinned. 'I get it.'

'You wait.'

'Bet it won't happen.'

'Ha, bet it will.'

'Well, not judging by the number of hot dates I've had this year.'

A bubble of laughter grew in her chest. 'You know people will start to talk about you if you're not careful.'

Ryan huffed. 'You mean more than they already do?'

'You're the one loving living in a wee small town.'

'It has its bad points too. Anyway, what exactly will they say? No, no, let me guess.' There was silence for a moment. *'How can someone that wonderful manage to stay single for so long?'*

Molly laughed at his vocal impersonation of a woman.

He continued, 'No, maybe something more like *Ryan Callaghan is a powerful good-lookin' hunk of a man isn't he?* That what you mean?'

'No.' She laughed again. 'I was thinking of you managing to stay single for so long and the fact that your best friend is a woman....'

'O'Brien, you better not be suggesting that I'm anything less than a hundred per cent red-hot male or I'll have to fly over there to show you different!'

'That'll be the day.'

'I'd spoil you for anyone else.'

'Sure you would.'

They smiled at each other from either side of the Atlantic. Molly thought for a moment or two, considering whether to tell Ryan about Kieran. Had enough time gone by?

'I've spoken to him, you know.'

Silence.

'Hello, over there—you still with me?'

'I'm here. You spoke to Kieran?'

'Uh-huh.'

'And how'd that go?' Ryan found himself holding his breath.

'Okay. At least we were able to talk like two adults, which is good.'

'He ask you to come back?'

Molly frowned at the cool edge to his voice. 'Aren't you the one always asking me if I'm sure I made the right choice?'

'Yeah, but aren't you the one always telling me it's over?'

'It is.'

'Then how come you spoke to him after all this time?'

She sighed. Ryan obviously wasn't ready to hear everything. She could tell by his tone. Maybe she'd never tell him—just let him believe that she'd broken Kieran's heart and it was all her fault.

'He wrote to me, and after the things he said in the letter I had to talk to him. There were…issues that needed dealing with, that's all.'

Ryan thought for a moment. Issues? What kind of issues? But then if Molly wanted to tell him she'd tell him. 'You're okay, though?'

'I'm fine—really.'

'You know you broke his heart, don't you?'

Molly sighed. 'Yes, I'm sure I did, and I'm sure he's sorry it didn't work out. But that's life. It's awkward for you, though. I'm sorry if you feel you're stuck in the middle.'

'Hey, don't go worrying about me. I'm a big boy now. I can dress on my own and everything.'

A smile. 'Hmm, I've seen how you dress. I wouldn't go boasting about it if I were you.'

There was silence for another moment, then he said, 'I'm not taking any sides here. You know that, don't you?'

'I know.'

'Good. Then about this red-hot male thing…'

'We need to talk.'

Molly turned at the sound of the familiar voice. She smiled wryly. 'I was wondering how long this was going to take.'

He had found her at her familiar thinking spot, in the Folly by the lough shore. When he'd gone to the shop to find her he had seen her walking towards the round stone building, lost in her own thoughts. And with an instinct born of familiarity he'd known that was where she would go.

'It had to happen some time, though.'

'Yeah, it did.'

Closing the distance between them with a couple of steps, Kieran enclosed her in his arms. Resting his chin on her head, he breathed in the familiar scent of her hair and smiled. 'How is it you always manage to smell so good?'

'Deodorant is a wonderful thing, Kieran, you should try it.'

His chest rumbled with low laughter. 'Lord, but I've missed you. Why haven't you come to see me since that first time you came home?'

Molly pulled back slightly from him so that she could smile into his familiar eyes. 'Hey, I could say the same thing, you know. I haven't seen you clocking up the miles on that flash car of yours to come see me either.'

'I guess I could try blaming work, or my new relationship with Neave, but somehow that's just not an excuse, is it?' He leaned towards her to whisper, 'How about I just say I'm sorry, and I should have visited more?'

Molly laughed. 'Then I guess an apology like that would work and I'd forgive you.'

'One of the things I loved about you the most was how understanding you were.'

'Well…' she moved away from him '…most times anyway.'

They looked at each other for a few silent moments. Molly was the first to break the tension, turning her back to look over the lough. 'Just in case I haven't said it, I'm really pleased about you and Neave.'

'Really?'

She turned round to face him again. 'Yeah, really. Just 'cos things didn't work out with us doesn't mean I don't still care about your happiness. She's perfect for you.'

His grey eyes glanced over her shoulder. 'Yeah, she is that.'

'But?'

'How did you know there was a but?'

Her laugh was brittle. 'Because I know you, and there was a but coming in that sentence.'

Kieran looked back into her eyes for a moment, then continued his study of the lough over her shoulder. 'Maybe it's just being here, where we all had so much fun. Those were happy times with you, Ryan and me. Being here has me thinking about that.'

A smile. 'They were great times.'

'Maybe it's got something to do with watching you and Ryan.'

Molly's stomach churned. Was this a confrontation?

'The thing is…' He shifted on his feet slightly. 'You two

still have as much fun together as we did back then, and I miss that. I guess what I'm saying is—'

'We can't be the people we were in university for the rest of our lives, Kieran.'

He looked irritated for a second, her words touching a nerve. 'I realise that, but I would just like some of that happiness back. Some of the joy we used to have in life. You and me.'

'Kieran.' Her eyes widened with questions. 'It's only natural that you're nervous about getting married; it's a very big step. But when you love someone enough to propose...'

'I proposed to you once.'

His quiet words still had the power to hit her midriff with the force of a kick. It was a lifetime ago now. And the girl who had been so in love with him then was not the same woman who had come home from the States after six years of running away. Any more than he was the same boy that she'd loved way back then.

Molly had grown up. She had learned from her mistakes and moved on. She had resolved her past with Kieran and got to know herself. But, truth be told, she'd never completely had 'closure' with Kieran. Never quite got over the fact that she could love someone that much and still have him cheat on her. Had he known she was falling out of love with him? Was that why he'd done it? Her sense of paranoia had even made her wonder if it had been her fault. Hadn't she been enough for him? And when two people had everything that they'd had in the beginning, how could it all fall apart? The thoughts made her angry even now.

'That was different.'

Kieran was surprised by the chill in her voice. 'Was it?'

'Look, Kieran, if you're afraid that Neave will run off like I did, then don't be. Unless you're dumb enough to mess things up again—which I'm sure you're not. This woman loves you in the ''rest of her life'' kind of way that you deserve. She knows you and loves you for the person you are right here and now. Not for the memory of a boy that you used to be.'

'And you don't?'

She sighed. 'Kieran—'

'No, come on. I'm curious. We were together for five and a half years, knew each other better than anyone else ever could, and yet it wasn't enough, was it? So what would it have taken, Molly? If I hadn't cheated on you would you still have left?'

'Don't do this.'

'I have to.' He ran his fingers through his light brown hair. 'I need to know that there's no possible chance for us before I jump into something else.'

Molly stared at him. 'You're *engaged*, for crying out loud. I'd have said that was you pretty much jumped clean into the middle of ''something else''.'

'I need to know before it goes any further.'

'Kieran, please. Leave this alone. It's a lifetime ago now, and we've managed to get through it and be friends—*just*.'

'Have we?'

One hand ran roughly across her eyes to clear her head. She'd taken a break from work to think about what had happened the night before with Ryan, and all of a sudden she was confronted with the problems of another relationship. It never rained...

'Look, we've stayed in touch with each other, we've never stopped caring—isn't that miracle enough, Kieran? What happened doesn't change our history. You don't care for someone that long and then just forget the emotion overnight. I'm sad that it didn't work, but it's in the past. It's done with.'

'Then how come you've not had another serious relationship since us? Hasn't that thought ever crossed your mind?'

If only he knew. 'That's none of your business.'

'It is if it means we should give us another try. What if we're meant to be, Molly? We could be throwing away a lifetime of happiness without even knowing.'

She stared at him for several moments, speechless. How could he even be saying this? It was something she had never, ever thought about, but Kieran had obviously given it a lot of thought. Maybe too much. She couldn't deal with this. Not now. Not now that Ryan…

Her eyes widened as she realised she couldn't tell Kieran what was happening with Ryan. He really wasn't ready to hear it. Any idea that she might have had about not actually hurting him after all this time, now that he had Neave…

Well, it was obvious that it *would* hurt him. And, much as she knew *she* could live with that, she was equally convinced that Ryan couldn't. He couldn't kill a spider, for crying out loud.

She shook her head. How long could they keep hiding it from Kieran? How could she explain this to Ryan? He shouldn't be made to think that she felt what had happened was some dirty little secret to hide. It had been the most amazing moment. So very precious already.

Kieran had stepped closer, his hand reaching towards her. 'Please, at least think about what I'm saying. Think about how happy we were. The three musketeers, remember?'

Not for much longer. Not if she asked Ryan to choose between Kieran and herself. Not that she doubted Ryan wanted her. Just that she knew he would never forgive her for hurting someone else to keep what she wanted for herself. She stepped back. 'I can't do this, Kieran. I can't talk about this with you. It's not fair to…'

He kept moving towards her. 'We need to know so that we can move on with our lives. *Together*, Molly.'

'No!' She pushed past him and did what she'd done just over six years earlier. She ran.

It was too much. Molly knew she couldn't deal with it. Everything was already too new and fragile, and in that moment she hated Kieran for making things more difficult.

She was still running ten minutes later when she collided with Ryan in the main foyer by his office.

'Oooof!'

His strong arms encased her and he stepped back with one leg to stop them both from falling over. 'Whoa, now. I know you're always keen to see me but, really, there's no rush. I'd still have been here after lunch.'

Breathless for a moment, she looked upwards into his smiling face and was horrified to find herself welling up. She tried to struggle free.

'I'm sorry.'

He saw the tears before she looked away. 'Hey, what's wrong?'

She laughed nervously. 'Nothing, really. You know us women. Always on the verge of some emotional crisis or another.'

'Crap.'

'What?'

'I said crap.' He tightened his hold when she continued trying to struggle free. 'You are the least emotional person I know.'

Molly managed to look annoyed through her tears. 'Well, thanks a bunch!' She thought for a moment. 'I think.'

'Tell me.' He raised an eyebrow.

Concern was the very last emotion she could deal with at that moment. At least from Ryan.

She shook her head, her hair flicking against her shoulders. 'I can't. Not right now. Please.'

A movement caught her eye through the foyer's large windows. She saw Kieran walking towards the building. 'I have to go.'

He noted the direction of her glance, the source of her impending departure, and his concern grew to the size of a small continent. 'What's going on?'

She noticed the soft tone of his voice, the determination in his eyes. 'Not now, Callaghan.' Again she struggled to get away.

'I think I have a right to know, don't you?'

'As my concerned friend or my jealous lover?'

'As both.' His gaze was sure and steady.

Molly looked around, noting the glances of a few surrounding tourists. 'Not here. Later.'

His arms tightened slightly in a reassuring hug. 'Tell you what, then, go out with me? Just the two of us. Like a real live couple. You can tell me your troubles and I'll try to take your mind off whatever it is.'

The suggestion in his low tones brought a smile to her face. Trust him to make her smile again. He'd always had that knack.

'Okay.' She glanced around again. 'Only if you *let go*.'

He released her with a slight smile. Watching her walk away, he thought for a moment about what was upsetting her. The paranoid voice in the back of his head wanted to know why Kieran still had the power to upset her at all—and, again, why she didn't want Kieran to know about their relationship.

Worse still, maybe it was he, Ryan, who had upset her in some way. Was she regretting what had happened between them? Hell, what if she hadn't enjoyed it as much as he had? A memory entered his mind of soft female cries and he smiled. Nope, that wasn't it.

Then he thought about what she'd said before she left. 'Only if you let go.' Ryan realised that he was fast approaching the stage of not wanting to do that. At least, not this time.

The 'date' was the perfect distraction.

After leaving a note at the shop in the afternoon for Molly to meet him at the lough's small harbour at seven, Ryan had done everything in his power to ensure things were just right. They had sailed across to one of the smaller islands and had a picnic dinner, and now sat watching the water lap against the shoreline.

'You know something?' Molly leaned back against his chest, a glass of wine in her hand. 'You remind me of someone I thought I knew.'

'Good looking, was he?'

She smiled. 'Passable.'

'Incredible sense of humour?'

'Mildly amusing at times.'

There was a slight pause. Then his words tickled softly against her ear. 'Terrific kisser?'

She turned to gaze up at him. 'I didn't know back then.'

'Wish you had done?' He kissed the end of her nose.

'My life was complicated enough at the time. Thanks, anyway.'

Ryan was silent for a moment, looking down at her face. 'Do you ever wonder what would have happened if things had been different?' He placed a light kiss on her mouth.

Molly set her glass onto the ground beside them, squirming around so that she lay looking up at him. 'Sometimes. Fairly recently sometimeses, actually.'

'We might never have met, never been friends. You

might never have dated Kieran. You might never have gone to the States.'

She sat up, this time facing him.

He continued, 'You wouldn't have had to make a homecoming and you and I wouldn't be lovers right now.'

Green eyes stared into chocolate-brown as he reached forward to brush a long lock of hair behind her ear. His fingers trailed along the side of her cheek before tracing her mouth.

'I want you to know I have no regrets about anything that's happened between us during any of the time I've known you,' she said.

His fingers trailed down over her chin, along the front of her neck, while his lips curled into a relieved smile. One doubt down.

'I'm not ashamed of what happened between us last night.'

His fingers moved over the rounded neck of her sweater, turning over to allow his knuckles to touch the soft skin he found there.

'It's called making love.' He smiled seductively at the question in her eyes. 'You referred to it as sex last night. I know the difference. What we did wasn't just sex. That may be a cliché, but it's the truth.'

Her chest rose and fell a little faster beneath his knuckles. 'I know that.'

'Good.'

She moved her hand up to where his lay against her skin and twined her fingers with his. 'Really, though.'

Moving his other hand to cup the back of her head, he drew her forward for a long, sensual kiss, igniting her senses again. 'I'm glad. 'Cos when it happens again I need to know you know what it is we're doing.'

Molly caught the teasing light in his eyes and rose to the bait. 'Oh, and we're going to do it again, are we?'

'Oh, yeah.'

'You mean that one time wasn't enough for you?'

'Now, woman, if you think for one minute that what we did has me wanting you any less then you're sorely mistaken.'

'Well then.' A sense of femininity swept over her bones. An old-fashioned sense of sexuality. It was basic, sensual, and really rather an all-round good feeling. She leaned forward and spoke against his mouth. 'Now that that's sorted out, maybe you should talk less and kiss more.'

He looked upward, as if thinking for a moment, then, 'Okay.'

Molly had thought that once they'd made love the spark in her belly wouldn't be so quick to fire up when he kissed her. But she had been wrong. If anything, the knowledge of what he was capable of doing to her body made it burn all the faster. The flames licked across her body and low into her abdomen as his tongue danced an age-old dance with hers. It felt so good. How could she ever have fought against something that felt this good? The odds were stacked against her. Hell, why would she even want to fight?

Their mouths tangled for long, glorious minutes before they eventually tore themselves apart for much-needed air.

Ryan brushed her hair back from either side of her face, kissing her forehead gently before resting his there. 'You want to tell me yet?'

Her eyes looked up into his, so close to her own. Ryan saw the inner debate and waited patiently. If she was going to tell him he wanted it to be her choice. Just as it always had been throughout their friendship.

'We used to talk about problems all the time, didn't we?'

He smiled. 'Indeed we did.'

'You were a remarkably good agony aunt for a guy.' She smiled in return.

'C'mon, O'Brien, if you can't talk to your best friend when you've a problem then who do you talk to?'

Molly moved her head away from him a little, her eyes never leaving his. 'It was different then. We weren't…we weren't doing all this.'

'Shouldn't the fact we're doing "all this" mean we talk more?'

'Technically…'

'So what's the difference? Why is this so difficult for you?'

She took a deep breath. 'This concerns Kieran.'

Ryan felt the temperature around them drop. He leaned away from Molly without even realising he'd done it. The paranoid voice in his head got louder. 'I'm listening.'

CHAPTER EIGHT

MOLLY noticed the moment he moved away from her. Not just physically either. It was almost as if a shutter came down over his eyes. For a moment she felt lost.

But she had spent the entire afternoon thinking about nothing else and had decided that she *needed* to tell him—because if she didn't he would overreact when he found out on his own. The phrase 'a rock and a hard place' had come to mind.

She took a deep breath. 'He came to talk to me.'

'That's nice. You two can't have had that deep a conversation since you came home.'

'We haven't.'

'So he decided to catch up on everything in your life and you told him about us.' He folded his arms across his chest. 'Right?'

Molly blushed. 'Not exactly.'

The voice in his head got louder. 'So you talked about, what? The weather?'

'No.' She noted the sarcasm in his voice, a harsh edge she'd never come across. 'He—he has some…doubts about his engagement to Neave.'

Ryan stared. *Stay calm, Ryan, stay calm.*

'He's not entirely sure if he's ready to get married to her.'

Dark eyes stared coolly into green. 'And you told him it was only natural he'd have doubts. But he'd be just fine.'

She nodded, clasping her hands unconsciously in front of her.

'So that was that, then.' He began clearing away the remnants of their food. 'Great. We'll send a nice gift and maybe you'll have got round to telling him that we're involved so that we can hold hands or something at the wedding.'

'It's not quite that simple.'

The voice in his head yelled *told you so,* and Ryan frowned, unable to look at her any more. 'Why?'

'He wants to know if we—he and I—' she swallowed hard in an attempt to moisten her dry mouth '—would stand a chance together. Before he settles down.'

There was a deadly silence everywhere except in Ryan's head. That was that, then. He would never stand a chance against that kind of history. What they'd had was years old and this was new and fragile. It hurt in a physical 'rip my guts out with your bare hands' kind of way.

He continued packing their things away.

Molly watched him. Of the many reactions she'd imagined him having, as she'd played the scenario in her head that afternoon, silence was not one of them. It scared her more than anything else could have.

'Callaghan?'

He stood up and began walking towards the small sailboat.

'Callaghan,' Her voice was louder, maybe even a little nervous. '*Talk* to me!'

He stretched to his full height, then turned slowly to face her. His face was expressionless, his eyes cold. 'What do you want me to say?'

Molly got angry. 'Something—anything at all that might indicate you give a damn would be quite good!'

'He's supposed to be my friend too, you know.'

'I know only too well.'

'So I'm hardly likely to go beat him to a pulp because

he still wants you. In fact, I can see more closely where he's coming from now.'

Her sharp intake of breath tapped the door to his conscience. His last statement had been uncalled for, and even he knew it. 'I'm sorry, O'Brien, that was harsh of me.'

The hurt shone in her eyes. 'You think?'

'I just don't get what it is you expect me to do here.' He held his hands out to his sides. 'You come out on a date with me, we spend the evening like any normal couple, and then you tell me you're going back to your ex. Who, incidentally, just happens to be my friend. What do you want me to say to you?'

As she stared at him he shook his head and turned away.

'I don't remember saying I was going back to him.'

There was another deafening silence.

'All I said was that he asked me whether or not we should try again. I just wanted to tell you before he came to talk to you about it—which I'm pretty sure he will.'

Ryan heard the sadness in her voice and his heart twisted in his chest. He'd overreacted, allowing the damn voice in his head to win. But he still knew that Molly and Kieran had a history. He'd seen them in love back then, when they'd been happy. Maybe Kieran was right. Maybe they did stand a chance of being together. But that didn't mean Ryan wanted it to happen. He was acting like a selfish idiot and he knew, when he thought clearly for a moment, that it wasn't helping his cause any.

'What do you want?'

Molly swallowed down the sob threatening to rise out of her chest. 'I want my life to not be so complicated.'

A nod. 'I can agree with that idea.'

'Ryan.' She reached out towards him, hesitated, and then touched his arm. 'Look at me.'

With a steadying breath he turned, and was floored by

what he saw in her eyes. She looked absolutely terrified. Without thinking about anything else he reached out to touch her cheek. 'You look like the world's about to end.'

'I can't lose my best friend.' She turned her face closer to his touch. 'I want to be honest with you, but how can I keep doing that if every time I tell you something difficult you walk away from me? I need you to talk to me through this because I don't know where we're going any more than you do.'

'You're not on your own.'

'Then don't walk away from me.'

With a sigh she stepped forward into his arms. Resting her cheek against his chest, she listened for the steady, reassuring beat of his heart.

'This is tougher than I ever thought it would be.'

Molly smiled at his words. She knew it had taken a lot for him to say them. Words weren't his thing. In all the years she had known him he had never been one to flaunt his emotions. She had never had to doubt that he cared because he worked passionately for the things he cared about. First his family, then his friends, his 'causes', and now the town he loved so much and his work at the park. They were the things that mattered most to him. He showed how much he cared through actions, not words. Trouble was, they were rapidly getting to the point where a few words were needed.

'Don't shut me out.'

He stroked her hair. 'What about Kieran?'

'Give it time. He'll see that Neave's the girl for him and this will all blow over.' She looked up, eyes shimmering. 'But 'til he does—'

'You still don't think he should know about us.'

'No.'

'Then we'll not discuss it again.'

Molly felt a small pang of unease. But rather than risk another confrontation on the subject she nodded her head. Things would be better when Kieran and Neave went home. And until then they just wouldn't discuss it.

Kate was completely stunned at Molly's reaction.

'What the hell do you mean, you entered me in the contest?'

'Aw, come on, Molly. You'll be a sure bet to win. You tell me who else would make a better Lady of the Lake?'

Molly saw red. 'How about someone who gives a damn?'

Kate looked even more surprised. 'Now, don't you think you're overreacting just a wee bit? It's all a bit of fun—like the bachelor auction.'

'What bachelor auction?'

'The one that Kieran entered Ryan in....' Her words slowed as she realised what Molly's reaction might be to that statement. 'But you knew about that, right?'

Molly's eyebrows practically disappeared beneath her fine fringe. 'Kieran entered *Ryan* in a bachelor auction? What exactly happens in this auction?'

Kate cleared her throat. 'Well, all the local women get to bid on the bachelors for a date....' she grimaced at her own words '...with them. Oh, dear.'

Molly gaped at her. 'Women get to bid for a date with Ryan. Women like Maura, right?'

'Like I said—oh, dear.'

'You aren't joking.' She thought for a moment, then started to laugh. 'Oh, dear, indeed.'

Kate placed a hand to the ache at the base of her spine and frowned at her mad friend. 'What's so funny?'

'He'll hate that so much.'

'And you won't have any problem with it, right?'

Molly was still giggling at the thought of Ryan's expression while being 'auctioned'. She then stopped to think of Maura, or any other willing female throwing themselves at him on a date, and her laughter turned to a frown. 'Oh, dear.'

'You could bid on him yourself. The local gossips would think that was just lovely.'

Molly grimaced, shaking her head. 'Uh-uh.'

Kate sat down an available stool. 'Oh, the whole Kieran thing, right? I take it he still doesn't know?'

'Nope.' She glanced at her friend's discomfort. 'You okay?'

'Oh, I'm grand. This baby feels like it weighs five tons but apart from that, I'm fine.'

Molly moved across to the kitchen counter to fill a glass with water. It was a rare occasion, now that Kate was so large, for them to spend a day shopping together. But they'd managed a Bank Holiday Monday in the larger local city of Sligo. It had been a carefree day of laughter and banter, but had cost Molly a blister and Kate even more swollen ankles than usual.

'Here.' She handed her the glass. 'Just think of how light and airy you'll feel when you have him or her. *Him* or *her?*'

Kate laughed. 'Your guess is as good as mine. We're waiting.'

'I don't know if I could stand the suspense.'

'Do you want kids, Molly?' She watched her friend's reaction over the rim of her glass.

Molly thought for a moment, staring into the middle distance. 'I guess so. I haven't really thought too much about it. When I was with Kieran we were too young to think about it—well, in the beginning anyway.'

'I always thought you two would get married and live

happily ever after. Instead here you are with Ryan. Life's funny, isn't it?'

'Oh, yeah, just hilarious.'

'I never understood what happened.'

Molly smiled at Kate, then walked over to the counter to hoist herself up onto its warm wooden surface. 'I bolted thousands of miles to get away. Didn't I ever mention that?'

'That I noticed. But why?'

'I don't know.'

Kate looked surprised, her delicate features forming a frown 'Aw, come on. You must know.'

A shrug. 'I loved him—at least I thought I did. We'd been together for a long time, and he even wanted to get married. I guess I just felt it wasn't right.'

'I didn't know he'd proposed. And *you* ran.'

'Mmm.'

Kate pounced. 'There's more than that though, isn't there?'

Molly stared at her, pursing her lips. Then she nodded.

'He cheated on you, didn't he?'

She wasn't surprised by Kate's knack for hitting the nail on the head. At least, not any more. 'Yeah, he did.'

'Bastard.'

'Kate! That baby can hear you, y'know.' Molly laughed.

Kate shrugged. 'I never did like Kieran. You deserved better. You don't still love him?'

Molly quirked an eyebrow. 'As the saying goes, I'm not *in love* with him. But I do still care—some. We were together for a long time before he got wandering eyes. You can't just forget that overnight. The things I felt then are all part and parcel of the things that made me who I am now.'

'What does Ryan have to say on the cheating subject?'

She dropped her chin. 'He kinda doesn't know that bit.'

'I bet he'd kill Kieran if he knew.'

'Yeah, well, I just left that bit out. He thinks that it was all me and I broke Kieran's heart. I wasn't going to be responsible for his losing his friend.'

Kate sighed. 'Oh, the tangled webs we weave.' She sipped at her water, her expression thoughtful. It was the first time they'd really discussed Molly's leaving since she'd come home, but it was obvious she had been hiding something from back then. Ryan had always been secretive, so she'd never known what he felt on the subject of the great break-up, but it had crossed her mind that he might not have been too upset about it. 'Are you sure you're not telling Kieran about you two because you're still a little in love with him?'

'Kate!'

Kate shrugged her shoulders elegantly. 'Well, it just occurred to me, and I'm sure it's bound to have occurred to Ryan.'

'You think I'd get involved with Ryan while I was still in love with Kieran?'

'No, but a man on unsure ground might think it. Especially if he didn't know the truth, the whole truth and nothing but the truth.'

The porch door opened and a smiling Neave arrived. 'Hi, there, how was the shopping trip?'

'Exhausting.' Kate groaned dramatically. 'And complete torture watching this one—' she pointed a finger at Molly '—trying on all those sexy dresses.'

Neave sat down next to Kate, her face open and animated. 'Find anything nice?'

Molly tried to avoid the woman's brown eyes, guilt eating her for no obvious reason. It wasn't as if she'd tried to steal her fiancé. But still, she knew that Kieran was having doubts and Neave didn't, and that made her feel lower than a snake's belly.

Kate grinned broadly. 'Only the killer dress she's going to win the Lady of the Lake title in.'

'Kate,' Molly warned, 'I'm not entering that stupid contest and that's that.'

'Well, it's tomorrow night, so it's too late to get out of it now. And anyway, you don't want that Maura winning, do you? Think of the bee you can put in her bonnet when you win.' She continued to grin widely.

Neave joined Kate's team. 'Oh, you should, Molly. And I can help with your hair and make-up if you like.'

'What's this for?' Kieran joined them, his eyes skimming over Molly's face. He noted the flush to her cheeks, then quickly looked away.

'Molly's entering the Lady of the Lake contest,' Neave gushed at him. 'It's tomorrow night.'

'What's tomorrow night?'

Molly groaned and dropped her face into her hands. 'Great.'

Ryan smiled at the crowd assembled in his kitchen before he launched himself up onto the counter by Molly. He did it without thinking, only remembering he shouldn't have when Kieran eyed him suspiciously. He nudged Molly in the ribs, then winked. 'Anything that makes Molly this uncomfortable has got to be good for a laugh or two—right, Kieran?'

Molly raised her face from her hands to glare at him. 'That's right. You take *their* side. I'll just fend for myself, oh, great protector.'

She smiled at him, seeing exactly what he was doing.

Her eyes told him that he had done well, and he smiled back at her. 'O'Brien, the only thing I have to protect you from is you. And your knack for taking things too seriously.'

'Oh, right. And you're just Mr Life's Too Short, aren't you? You're Mr Leave All Responsibility Behind and Live for the Moment. That's why you got a job here and settled down like a crusty old bachelor.' She nudged him back.

'What can I say? When you find your niche…'

Molly smiled affectionately. 'You got lucky, is all.'

He couldn't miss the innuendo in her words, and his eyes sparkled. 'You aren't joking either.'

Kate smiled at their easy banter, then realised who their audience was. With a quick sideways glance she could see the wheels turning in Neave's head and a frown appearing on Kieran's face. 'You two just crack me up. You're always making fun of each other. With friends like that who needs enemies, right?' She smiled at Neave.

Neave smiled back. 'I think it's cute.'

Ryan pointed two fingers towards his open mouth, pretending to be sick. 'Ughh.'

Another poke in the ribs. 'That's what you get for taking their side, you see. They turn on you.'

One dark eyebrow raised in curiosity about the original subject of their conversation. 'Ah, yes—what was that about, anyway?'

'Kate, with the hormonally warped mind of a pregnant lady, decided to enter me in the Lady of the Lake contest.'

Ryan grinned broadly, lighting up the room 'Good girl, Kate.'

Molly laughed as he managed to avoid another poke in the ribs. 'I should have known you'd find that funny, you great lump.'

'And you should see the dress she got for it.' Kate wiggled her eyebrows at the audience. 'Why, the thing is so hot it'd burn your eyes!'

'Kate!'

'Well, I can't wait.' Ryan glanced round at Molly again. 'Will it make you look more like a girl?'

She looked down at her loose grey trousers and sweatshirt, then back into his shining eyes. 'Get lost, you!'

Ryan's laughter erupted from deep in his chest.

Blinking slowly for a moment, she humoured him before raising her chin defiantly. 'And I'm glad you find it so very funny. We'll just see how funny tomorrow looks to you when you go under the hammer, friend.'

He frowned in mock confusion. 'All right—now you've lost me.'

Molly folded her arms neatly across her chest and smiled at Kieran. 'Why don't you tell him about it, Kieran?'

Kieran stared at her for a moment. Then he looked at Ryan, then back at Molly. 'I'd hate to spoil your fun. Why don't you tell him?'

She tore her eyes from his cool stare and looked into the warmth of Ryan's eyes. 'He entered you into the bachelor auction.'

She could have sworn he went pale beneath his tanned skin.

'No way.'

A nod. ''Fraid so.'

Kate laughed in the background. 'I swear, if I go into labour between now and tomorrow night I'm going to cross my legs. I wouldn't miss this for the world.'

Christmas—two years earlier

'These travellers' children have every much a right to an education as other kids do!'

The town council watched silently as Ryan stood his ground. 'Just because they don't live in a neat semi-detached house it doesn't mean they should be treated any differently.'

Patrick Kennedy, town mayor, looked over the rim of his glasses. 'No one's trying to treat them any differently, but the fact is their families don't pay any taxes—so how can we put them into a school funded by taxes?'

'That school barely has enough children in it to fill two rooms. How can ten more children make that big a difference?' Ryan shook his head, a frown firmly in place. 'For dear's sake, man, some of them are only six years old. How much can it cost to teach them to read and let them colour in some pictures?

Molly sneaked quietly into a seat at the back of the council meeting rooms and watched. She'd wanted to surprise him with her Christmas visit and instead had been surprised by him not being home. The night guard at the park had directed her towards the Town Hall. 'He's standin' up for some kids or somethin', I think.'

A smile crossed her lips as she watched him in action. Another cause. Ryan wouldn't be Ryan if he weren't fighting for the things he thought mattered. Standing up to be counted was how he showed he cared.

'The fact remains that we can't have some people paying towards their children's education and other people not.'

Ryan shrugged. 'Discrimination being much better, of course.'

Celia Farrelly, upstanding council member, looked outraged. 'Mr Callaghan, I hardly think that's fair.'

'Well, that would be the definition of discrimination, Mrs Farrelly. Hardly fair.'

The woman positively bristled at him. 'I don't think this is the time for hilarity, Mr Callaghan.'

'Neither do I, Mrs Farrelly.' He looked back at the mayor. 'Look, Mayor, if it makes the council sleep easier in their beds at night you can bill me for the children's share of reading books and crayons. Fair enough?'

The mayor looked appeased. 'We would, of course, make sure that that fact was made known to the school board and the children's parents. So they can thank you, Ryan.'

Ryan shook his head. 'Oh, no, you don't. Those are proud people. They'll see it as charity and I don't want that.' He smiled coolly. 'Why don't you just go right ahead and let them think you allowed it yourself? That should help the council's image, don't you think?'

The councillors glanced back and forward at each other. 'If that's how you want it...'

'It is.'

They gathered their papers and started to leave the room. Ryan sat for a moment, frowning at the empty table. How could so many people be so narrow-minded? He stood slowly, running his fingers through his hair as he turned. Boy, he was tired...

She smiled softly at him. 'Still wearin' those underpants outside your trousers, Callaghan?'

His eyes met hers and his face lit up. 'O'Brien!'

Inside two strides she was whisked up into a bear hug and swung in circles. 'Well, hell, it's good to see you.'

Molly giggled like a long-ago schoolgirl as he set her down. With a grin she stepped back out of his hold so that she could look at him. Outdoor work obviously suited him. He looked pretty darned good. Broad and tanned.

'What're you doing here?'

Linking her arm through his, she turned towards the double doors. 'Visiting you, you idiot. Why else would I visit this tiny place?'

He frowned down at her playfully. 'Hey, just you watch it, townie. This happens to be the place I call home. And I'm rather fond of it.'

'So the rumour goes.'

They stopped beside his Jeep while Ryan opened the door.

'My hire car's over there.' She nodded to the other side of the narrow street. 'Why don't we go to Riley's for a drink instead?'

'How long are you here for?'

'I don't know. As long as it takes for you to get sick of me, I guess.' She smiled again. It was good to be with him. Somehow occasional phone calls hadn't been enough.

His eyes sparkled in the light of the orange streetlamps. 'Well, you better just get right back in your car and go, then.'

'Ha, ha.' She laughed, despite her best efforts to keep a straight face. 'I've booked into the hotel for a couple of nights, and then I promised the folks I'd bring you home for Christmas.'

'The "folks"?' A grin. 'There you go, gettin' all American on us. Interesting accent, by the way.'

'And I'm visiting you because…?'

'Because—' he relocked the door, throwing his arm across her shoulders '—I'm the only one able to get you home to dear old Ireland.'

She smiled. 'Oh, is that so? How come?'

'Because deep down you love me more than anyone else and you just can't stay away from me.'

'Heck, Callaghan, how do you get your head through doors?'

He squeezed her closer to his side. 'One day you'll notice how charming I really am.'

'How do you know I haven't noticed already?'

'Well, you see…' he stopped and turned her to face him '…if you had then you'd be right here instead of halfway across the world.'

Molly lifted her chin. 'I'm here now, aren't I?'

Dark eyes searched hers with curiosity, his head tilted slightly. There was something different—something new. What was it? After several silent moments Molly smiled mischievously. 'Well, it's either that or all my other friends left the country this week. I can't remember which it was.'

'It's good to see you too, O'Brien.'

The knock on her door was so soft she barely heard it. Pulling back the light cover, she padded across the wooden floor on bare feet. On inspection she found Ryan leaning against her doorframe.

'What are you doing?' She glanced into the dark hallway while hissing the words at him. 'You'll get caught, you idiot!' He ducked down, lifting her into his arms before closing the door softly. 'I can't help it,' he whispered in her ear. 'I missed you.'

She smiled at him. 'You saw me not twenty minutes ago.'

'I know.' He laid her down on the wide bed, then lay beside her. 'But I still missed you.'

'You're sad.'

He looked up at her from beneath his dark eyelashes, pouting with his wide lower lip. 'Can I help it if I find you irresistible?'

Molly laughed softly. 'What am I going to do with you?'

'I can think of a few things.'

'I bet you can.'

He moved closer to her, his breath causing goosebumps along her arm. One hand reached up to allow long fingers to run through her hair. 'I've been thinking.'

'You shouldn't strain yourself like that.' She ran her fingers through his hair in return. 'I wouldn't want you to hurt anything.'

'Well, I've been thinking that maybe if we slept in the same bed we would get more sleep than we're getting at the minute.'

'How do you figure that one?'

He watched his hand as it ran from her hair along the length of her arm. '*I* can't seem to sleep because all I do is think about touching you, and while I'm not sleeping I can hear *you* moving about the house.'

Molly watched his face as he watched himself touching her. 'I can't seem to sleep too good either.'

A smile. 'So, if we slept where we could still touch each other then we would sleep more....'

Molly's heart twisted at the gentleness of his touch. The soft temptation of his words. He had the power to tug her heartstrings, she realised. When had that started? Had he always had that power over her? It was just that as he watched her with almost boyish fascination she was reminded of the teenager she'd known. While at the same time being so easily aroused by the man he'd become. It was a wondrous, magical thing.

'Don't you think we'd sleep even less *because* we'd spend the whole night touching each other?'

His body hardened immediately at the suggestion. 'That's a chance I'd be willing to take.'

His nightly growth of coarse beard grated under her fingernails as she caressed his strong jaw. He was irresistible to her too. Touching him was her favourite pastime and she just didn't care. How could something that felt this good not be absolutely right?

She slid further down the bed until her face was even with his. 'You have to promise not to make too much noise.' She brushed her lips against his. Her eyes staring into his, she watched for an amber spark of desire in their dark depths and was rewarded.

He watched the seductive smile that grew across her mouth and smiled back. 'I promise if you promise.'

Molly wrapped her arms around his neck, pushing her body tight against him. 'I've missed you too, Ryan.'

A heart-stopping kiss later he raised his head to smile. 'About this hot dress…'

'Mmm.'

'I don't suppose there's any chance of a sneak preview?'

'Uh-uh.' Her breathing quickened as his fingertips began exploring. 'Some things are best waited for.'

Without raising his head he looked up at her. 'I'll remember you said that.'

CHAPTER NINE

New Year—two years earlier

THEY spent nearly four days together in Boyle, despite Molly's schedule. But it was the most fun she'd had in a very long time. It made her remember all the things she'd loved about their holidays a lifetime ago. When he'd joked about being the only one who could convince her to come home to dear old Ireland she'd laughed it off. She was doing what she wanted to do in the States. She'd photographed wildlife, taken news shots for the local papers and was even managing a show of her work in a small San Francisco gallery. She was happy, settled and confident in herself. The world was just fine. Molly O'Brien was finally getting to know Molly O'Brien. And she didn't think she was all that bad.

After visiting her 'folks' for Christmas, Ryan had insisted on taking her to the airport for her flight back. 'Gives me more time to convince you to stay.'

They were early arriving, so sat in the food hall with huge mugs of cappuccino, watching the planes take off. Ryan told jokes about tourists and Molly pulled faces at the punchlines. But below the surface she wasn't smiling. Eventually the air between them grew still and quiet.

'Aw, hell, O'Brien, why don't you just put everyone out of their misery and come on home?'

'Don't start again.'

'Can't help it.' He looked down at his mug, then back

at her face, his cheeks displaying a slight flush. 'I miss having you around.'

His confession startled her. She blinked at him.

Ryan grinned. 'What? You didn't think I would?'

Molly shrugged. 'I didn't think much about it.'

'Well, thanks, friend.' He mock-grimaced.

'I just know you're here, and somehow that's enough for me right now.'

Dark, familiar eyes stared at her. 'You'll come back one day, O'Brien, and when you do I'll still be here, I'll still care. All you have to do is remember that. Maybe even think about it a bit.' Molly stared at him. Ryan Callaghan, her friend. She missed having him around too. But this visit had opened her eyes in ways that she hadn't been ready for before. She found herself looking at him, really looking. And every time she looked she got a warm sensation across her body. There was just no one else like him in the world. At least not for her. In many ways that was more frightening than anything else she had learned in her time away. It frightened her to death, and until she wasn't scared any more she knew she wasn't ready to come home. Almost as if by coming home she would have to give up something of herself.

The tannoy announced the boarding call for her flight.

In silence they gathered her bags and headed for the check-in desk. Once everything was checked through, and she had her boarding card, she turned to look at him. And found she couldn't. Pain gripped her chest and she had to swallow hard to remove the lump forming in her throat.

Ryan stared down at her bowed head, then reached out and raised her chin with one long finger. Her eyes shimmered up at him with unshed tears. 'Molly?'

She shook her head. Without thinking she threw her arms around his neck and hugged him tight. Words just seemed to be stuck in her throat. She couldn't get them out. So instead she tried to pull as much of his strength into her body as she could hold onto. How many times could she keep leaving home—and Ryan? Because behind everything else there was always Ryan.

They stood for what seemed like an eternity. Two best friends, saying their goodbyes. Then Ryan cleared his throat. 'Don't go.'

A tiny voice sounded against his neck. 'I have to.'

'I don't know if I can keep on saying goodbye to you.'

Molly sobbed. 'It's not time yet. I'll know when it is because I'll not be able to leave again.'

Then she pulled free and walked through the departure gates.

The first time he saw her 'hot dress' she was standing on a makeshift stage at the Riverside Hotel. Neave and Kate had whisked her off to their secret female domain straight after work and Ryan hadn't seen her before she left the house. So, instead of ogling her in the privacy of his own home, he found himself gaping at her in public. She took his breath away. Again.

The twelve contestants had filed onto the stage while he stood at the bar chatting to the barman. Only turning round when the presenter made his introduction, he had taken him a moment to find her.

Her vivid green eyes, made larger with the subtle make-up, searched him out in the crowd. When she found him she smiled, and his chest threatened to crush all the air out of his lungs.

'Wow.'

Her smile widened as she read his lips. When it was her turn to step up to the microphone she spoke looking at him. 'Hey, there. I'm Molly O'Brien, and as you may know I've come home, at last, after a long time away. It's *good* to be back.' She paused while there was a ripple of applause, her eyes seeking out Kate's rounded form. Then she added, 'I have to admit a friend entered me for this contest, but I also have to admit to her that it's been nice getting dressed up and seeing the look on people's faces. So thanks, Kate, but just remember—I owe you one!'

Ryan smiled affectionately at her threat, his eyes never leaving hers. Those women had done something to her hair. It was piled high on her head, with soft curls falling loose to frame her neck. It was sexy as all hell. But not as sexy as her dress.

The same green as her eyes, it had impossibly small shoelace straps and a low scooping neckline that shaped the fullness of her breasts. And, damn, but it was short. The woman had the longest legs in all creation, and his eyes darkened as he remembered them wrapped around him until late into the night. Yep, he was definitely a legs man.

'She looks amazing.'

Ryan dragged his eyes away from her when Kieran spoke. He looked at his profile and nodded calmly. 'Yeah, that she does.'

In silent agreement they turned to face the bar. Ryan ordered two beers and, bottles in hand, they turned back to watch the judging.

'I'm not blind, Ryan, so I'm just going to come out and ask you. How long have you been sleeping with her?'

Ryan's jaw tensed. He looked up at Molly's smiling face while she answered a question from the audience. He wouldn't lie, but… 'I don't think that's any of your business.'

Kieran looked at him from the corner of his eye. 'You are sleeping with her, though?'

Ignoring the question, he took a long draw from his beer

bottle. He'd known this would be uncomfortable. It was probably why he'd spent the day avoiding Kieran. Molly had been right when she'd assumed that Kieran would eventually come to talk to him. And Ryan had known that he really didn't want to listen if it involved Molly. So he'd avoided being alone with him.

'Look, Ryan, I don't want to get into one with you about this. I just need to know. ' Kieran turned towards him. 'I've been watching you two and it started to click with me that there was something going on.'

Ryan glared at him. 'It's still none of your business whether or not I'm sleeping with her.'

'Maybe not.'

He laughed sarcastically. 'No *maybe* about it.'

Kieran looked back at the stage. He thought for a moment, and then looked back at his friend. 'Did she tell you I had a talk with her?'

Ryan slowly grew taller in his shoes. He felt anger bubbling in the pit of his stomach and his eyes automatically searched for Molly's. She was looking from Kieran to him and back again, a small frown of concern on her face. When her eyes found his she raised one eyebrow in question. It was a silent language of looks that they had perfected over the years.

'She told me.'

'Then you know I want her back.'

His eyes stayed transfixed on Molly. So beautiful. She was just so beautiful to him. He'd never met anyone like his Molly, and he wasn't about to let go without a fight. God, he'd been in love with her most of his life, hadn't he?

But the damned voice was still there. It needed its questions answered, and he knew that even if his possessive side didn't want to admit it. Kieran and Molly were both his friends. What if they *were* 'meant to be'? Was he selfish enough to stand in the way of that?

Hell, yes. He wanted to yell it out. But he couldn't. Molly had unfinished business with Kieran and they all knew it. 'You better discuss that with her, Kieran.'

He took another long draw of beer and then stepped closer to the smaller man, his voice dangerously low. 'I'm telling you now, though. Unless *Molly* tells me she needs to find out things aren't over with you, I'm not walking away. And even then, if by some miracle you're lucky enough to get her back, I'll still be here, in the wings, waiting for you to screw up. If for any reason at all it doesn't work out I'll do my damnedest to get her back and keep her. You got me?'

Kieran looked surprised. 'I get you.'

Ryan's smile was cold. 'I'm only telling you the facts.'

'I have to find out, Ryan. I have to try and make things up with her. I need to know that letting her go wasn't the biggest mistake of my life. Surely you can understand that, now that you've been with her?' Kieran's smile was snide. 'And you're never going to be completely sure of her until you find out if she has any feelings left for me, *are you*?'

Ryan's focus returned to the stage. Although he had the strongest urge in the world to flatten Kieran where he stood, he also knew he was right. But knowing he was right and letting go were two different things. All he knew was that he loved Molly and he wanted what would make her happy. If she had any feelings left for Kieran then he would have to let her go. That much was a given. He only hoped by letting her go she'd eventually realise that Kieran was wrong for her, and that he, Ryan, was her Mr Right after all.

'I've never danced with a beauty queen before.'

Molly raised her chin indignantly. 'I'm not a beauty

queen. I'm the Lady of the Lake. There's a difference, y'know.'

Ryan nodded wisely. 'Of course there is.'

He swung her round in a wide circle, drawing laughter from her lips. He liked dancing with Molly. It was the closest he could get to making love to her in public. His hand splayed across the small of her back as he drew her closer. 'By the way, have I mentioned how very hot this dress is?'

She tangled her fingers in the hair at the nape of his neck. 'Not in the last five minutes or so.'

'Well, it is, you know.'

'Don't you think it shows a little too much leg?'

They both looked down at her legs. Ryan seemed to ponder a moment, then decided with a sigh, 'There is no such thing as too much leg.'

'Oh, is that right?' She laughed at his innocent look.

He nodded sagely, then grinned. 'Ooh, watch out—dip ahead.' To her surprise he leaned forward and dipped her backwards, his face leaning down towards her to grin even more. 'Gotta watch out for those dips.'

Molly laughed as he settled her back into an upright position. One hand moved from his neck to smooth down what there was of her skirt. 'Yeah, I can see how they'd be dangerous.'

Ryan wiggled his eyebrows. 'In that dress they're almost illegal.'

The music melded into another soft ballad and Molly tilted her chin to look up at him. 'Ready for the auction, are we?'

'Why? You bring your chequebook?'

'Who said I was bidding?'

He looked hurt. 'You'd let me loose amongst all those scary single women? How could you do that to me?'

'I'd insist on going on the date as your chaperon.'

'Phew!' He squeezed her a little tighter. 'And there I thought I'd have to leave the country to get away.'

That drew a laugh. 'No, I think you'll find that's my trick.'

He smiled softly down at her. 'Don't ever do that to me again—you hear, O'Brien?'

'Wouldn't you come get me this time?'

'I guess I'd have to know that you wanted to be got.'

Molly noted how his eyes moved away from her as he spoke. She frowned at the serious tone to his voice. Serious, and something else. Almost sad. But why?

'Don't you think you know me well enough by now to know whether or not I'd want you to come get me?'

Still he avoided her eyes. 'I'd hope that I did. But it might not be as simple as that.'

'Why not?'

'It might be better for you if I didn't—if I let you come home on your own.'

Molly blinked at him in confusion. 'What does that mean?'

'Maybe, like last time, I'd have to step back and wait until you'd found all your answers.'

'Answers to what?'

'O'Brien—'

'Ryan.' A hand appeared on Ryan's sleeve. 'We need you to get ready for the auction now.'

He released his hold on her, smiling as he walked away. 'See ya later, O'Brien.'

'Nice crown, Molly.' Kate grinned up at her.

Molly straightened the offending plastic item on her head, grimacing. 'Pinches a little.'

'Looks good on you, though.' Kate wiggled her finger. 'No taking it off for the rest of the evening.'

'I'll try not to.'

Sitting at the table with her friends, Molly glanced around the crowded room and noted the number of females that suddenly appeared. She frowned.

Kate grinned all the more. 'Good crowd in for the auction, isn't there, Molly?'

'Mmm.'

'They should get some good bids in, don't you think?'

'I guess.' Her eyes spotted Maura in the front row of tables. Molly thought horrible thoughts, then smiled. She'd never thought of herself as the 'keep your hands off my man' type. But somehow she suddenly understood where the emotion came from.

Kate edged forward on her seat, reaching out for a helping hand from Molly. 'Well, the baby's sitting on my kidneys so I'm off to pay a visit before this kicks off.'

'I'll join you.' Molly lifted her purse from the table, smiling sweetly at Neave and Kieran. 'Won't be long.'

Moments later Kieran was waiting for her when she walked into the narrow hallway behind the stage. He stepped towards her as she approached, noting the caution in her eyes. 'Going to see Ryan?'

'I thought I'd wish him luck, yes. He's going to hate every minute of this. As you rightly knew when you entered him for it.'

He smiled. 'I knew he wouldn't like it much, but then this was the kind of dumb prank we always pulled on each other at uni.'

Molly shook her head. 'You still spend every day wishing your life was like it was then, don't you?'

Kieran's face fell. 'But, Molly, everything was just so right then. It made sense. We all had so much fun in those days.'

She stared at him for a moment, stunned by the level of sympathy she felt for him. He was right, to a certain degree. They had been happy then. Everything had been so much simpler.

People had flocked around Kieran, attracted by the magnetism of his personality. And he'd had time for everyone—listening to their problems, making them laugh when they were down. Maybe that was part of the reason she'd been so attracted to him. He had been everything that at that time of her life she wasn't. Confident, vivacious, beautiful to look at. And maybe by being at his side, by having him love her, she had managed to have some of those qualities rub off onto her.

There was an uneasy silence between them as Kate and a few others squeezed past them. Kate glanced at Molly with a raised eyebrow and Molly nodded to her. 'I'm fine. You go sit down. I'll be right there.'

Kieran turned slightly to look at her profile. 'You've been avoiding me, haven't you?'

She sighed. 'Yes.'

'I haven't changed my mind, you know. I still think we should see if there's anything left between us. You have to know that I never stopped loving you, Molly. I just learnt to live without you.'

Molly turned wide eyes towards him. 'You went on with your life. It was what I'd hoped you do. It's what I did.'

His hand reached out to grasp hers. 'We were happy once. We could be happy again. I believe that.'

'Kieran—'

'I know about you and Ryan.'

His words stopped her in her tracks. He knew? How?

She remembered seeing him standing at the bar with Ryan. One plastic crown and suddenly she was an idiot. So the cliché about beauty contest winners struck yet again.

'He told you.' Her eyes sparked with anger. Was Kieran going to turn this to his advantage in some way? Ryan should have waited for her. They could have told Kieran together, and then he wouldn't have any way to twist the facts round....

'He won't stand in our way.'

She gaped at him.

'So, you see—it's okay. We can just walk away from the past few years and start again.' He squeezed her hand. 'I can forgive you for getting involved with him just like you forgave me for being such an idiot back then. After all, you're bound to have been curious after living with him for a while, and I did think things would be better with us if you just scratched that itch. So you were lonely, and being with him reminded you of all the good times. I understand. After all, it reminded me too.'

Ryan felt really stupid. First of all he was wearing a tuxedo, of all things. Why the organisers felt that was necessary he had no idea. The thing was truly uncomfortable and, if truth be told, a little on the tight side in certain areas. And he had just pretty much told Kieran that Molly could leave and restart their relationship while he waited in the wings. Sheer genius on his behalf, and an out and out lie. If Kieran honestly thought he wouldn't fight like hell to keep her when he had waited so long for her to be his, then he had another think coming.

Five minutes away from the auction he made a major decision. He was going to tell her how he felt. Really, this time. No chickening out and hiding behind being her friend.

No pretending to himself that he would get over it. Because he wouldn't.

With a grin on his face wide enough to light a room, he went looking for her.

'Molly?'

Kieran's voice was drowned out as loud rock music blasted out of the speakers. The house lights dimmed at the front of the stage and a spotlight wobbled its way to where the first of the bachelors was appearing.

'Hello, I'm Paul, and I'm worth every penny!'

There was a loud cheer from the audience and a ripple of laughter. The 'bachelors' had obviously been told to ham it up.

Kieran raised his voice. 'Molly, please. I need you to talk to me.'

'I'm Gerard. I'm looking for a romantic date with a fun girl.'

'I want to tell Neave tonight. I don't think it's fair to string her along any more.'

Molly's mind spun. So many pictures from her life flickering through her brain.

'Molly?'

Molly stared at him, suddenly realising several things. Kieran's words had made her think about why she was involved with Ryan Callaghan. Was it because he reminded her of a better time that she wanted to recreate? Was it because she'd always been curious about this other side of him? Was it because she was lonely?

'I'm in love with him.'

Kieran gaped at her. 'What?'

'My name's Pat and—'

Molly raised her eyes to look at him. 'I'm in love with Ryan.'

'No, Molly.' He reached for her hand. 'You may love him. I mean, he's been like a brother to you, but—c'mon. I mean, it's *Ryan*, for God's sake. You can't be in love with him.'

More 'bachelors' introduced themselves, and she almost had to yell as she answered him. 'I do, Kieran. I love him. I love him *because* he's Ryan. My best friend, my protector...' she smiled softly '...and my lover.'

She stepped back slightly from his outreached hand. 'And if I'm going to be completely honest with myself, and with you, then I should tell you that I was probably in love with him before I ever left. I just didn't know what it was I felt.'

Kieran stared. 'You don't mean that.'

She looked down at her hands and then back into his pale face. 'I never meant for it to happen, Kieran. I want you to believe that. But the more time I spent with him the more I was beginning to notice him, and it made me think about what I was doing. Then, every time I left him I left more of myself behind, until I had to come home to be whole again.'

'Did you sleep with him back then?'

His voice was so harsh she almost flinched. 'No, it wasn't like that. I didn't even know what it was I was feeling. So I did what I thought was best. I stayed away and tried to live my life. It's not that I'd lusted after him for years like some lovesick idiot. He just kind of crept up on me when I wasn't looking. But I really do love him— and, unlike you, I won't do anything to risk losing that.'

He smiled sarcastically. 'So you just waited six years and then came back to seduce him?'

Molly almost laughed at the very suggestion. But she knew that Kieran was hurting, so she bit her tongue and took a deep breath. 'I convinced myself it was just a kind of homesickness. I convinced myself it had never been there in the first place. But when I came home I came home because of him, Kieran. I came home *to* Ryan.'

'You lied.'

'I lied to myself.'

'And to me, when you didn't tell me you were sleeping with him.' He thought for a moment, then shook his head. 'No—don't you see? Why wouldn't you tell me about it if you didn't still care for me?'

'I do. I can't just erase what happened between us, and I'm sorry that you're so unhappy with your life.' It was Molly who stepped closer this time. 'We *both* care. And, for the record, it will cost Ryan a lot, knowing that we've hurt you.' She watched the flash of anger cross his face. 'We're not meant to be, you and I. Don't you see that?'

'Oh, and you and Ryan are?'

Molly sighed. 'Yes, I honestly believe we are.'

Kieran was silenced for a moment, his eyes searching hers for the truth. Then he seemed to make a sudden decision. With no warning he stepped forward and pushed Molly back against the wall. Her cry of protest was smothered by his mouth on hers, and Molly's hands moved up to his chest to push him away.

Ryan stood by the edge of the stage, staring into the hallway.

'Ryan, you can go on now.'

His dark eyes watched as Kieran kissed Molly. That was that, then. Too late once again. Good God, he'd never learn, would he? After all that had happened she could just waltz back to Kieran without a thought.

End of story.

With a blank glance at the stairs beside him, he walked onto the stage.

* * *

'What the hell do you think you're doing?' Molly yelled at Kieran as he released her. 'Have you completely lost your mind?' At least he had the grace to look embarrassed. 'He doesn't love you, Molly. Not the way you want.'

Molly closed her eyes for a moment. It was amazing how, when people sought to hurt the ones they loved, they always managed to pick on their deepest fears. 'Don't do this, please.'

'Would he be willing to let you go if he loved you that much? Would you be able to do the same in his shoes? Because, let me tell you, I wouldn't. *I won't.*'

Molly shook her head, moving away from him. She'd heard enough.

'He wouldn't come after you if you left him, you know. And if he felt the same way as you, wouldn't he have told you before now, fought for you? Isn't that what Ryan does, Molly?'

Words echoed in her recent memory. 'It might be better for you if I didn't,' he'd said.

'Surely if he loved you he'd fight for you—like *I* did before you finally left?'

Molly thought about how Ryan fought for the things he loved. Why *would* he let her walk away if he really loved her as much as she loved him? And she had loved him for as long as she could remember, looking back. Not loving Ryan would be like not breathing in and out.

'How long do you think this will last, Molly? We both know that Ryan has never stuck in any relationship for more than five minutes. He doesn't know how to.'

Would she let him go if the tables were turned? Could she have allowed her two friends to live happily ever after if she'd been in love with one of them?

'I guess I'd have to know that you wanted to be got,' he'd said.

Her chest ached. If he loved her there was no guarantee that it was the 'in love' kind of love. Wouldn't he fight to keep her if it were? Because she'd damn well fight for him. She'd want to know if he didn't feel what she felt. So that she could mend her heart and get on with her life. And that was what Ryan had been asking, in his own roundabout way. He 'guessed' he'd have to know if she wanted him to come and get her. He'd want to be sure she loved him completely before he'd take a chance. A guarantee that he wouldn't get hurt. Because when he loved, he loved with all his heart and soul. Just as he'd loved his parents. When he'd found out they were dead his world had ended. He'd shouted his anger at the universe, then dared the planet to take his life too, by risking his neck for his 'causes'. He'd then replaced pain with something else. Passion. Passion for the things he loved the most. The things he *wanted* the most.

Molly wanted his passion. Out of the bedroom *and* in it. She wanted him to fight for her harder than he'd fought before. Wouldn't he do that for her as a friend? *Yes.* Then why couldn't he do it as her lover? Unless…unless he didn't love her in the same way. It wasn't some kind of a contest that Molly wanted him to win. She wanted Ryan, body, heart and soul. With all that passion. If she couldn't have that…

'You'll only end up hurt and alone, and you don't want that.'

When she turned, her eyes were colder than he'd ever seen before. 'Shut up, Kieran. This is really none of your business any more. It stopped being your business who I loved the day you decided it would be okay to screw around. I got over that, now you need to get over this— and pray that Neave thinks you're worth it.'

Taking a shaky breath, she glared at Kieran. She knew

deep in her heart that it was probably the last time she would ever see him. It was just about time she closed that particular chapter of her life. Before sorting out the next one. 'If I were you, right now I would be running back out there showering as much love and attention on Neave as I could manage. You *really* don't deserve her, you know.'

'Molly—'

'No, you listen, Kieran. I'm talking now.' She stepped towards him, her eyes glittering with anger. 'You have spent far too many years wallowing in self-pity, don't you think? Most people would give their eyeteeth to have the start in life you had, but it was never enough for you. So just *go away*, Kieran. I don't ever want to see you again. Is that clear enough for you? No reunion, no happily ever after. Not with me anyway. Sort your life out.'

She glanced down, and then up, her eyebrow lifting in disdain. 'You really are quite pathetic, aren't you?'

CHAPTER TEN

RYAN was about to be 'auctioned' when Molly reappeared at the side of the stage. She smiled an encouraging smile at him, which was met with absolutely nothing. His face was closed to her for the first time ever.

'Go for it in the intro,' they'd told him offstage. Fine. That was what they wanted, that was what they'd damn well get.

'Ladies.' He smiled the most seductive of smiles. 'You all know who *I* am. Who can I tempt with an evening of *undivided* attention?'

With almost rehearsed ease he peeled off his jacket and slung it over one shoulder. He then reached up and loosened his bow tie. 'Who would like to spend one night with me?'

Women moved towards the stage in a wave of hypnotised faces.

'Fifty!'

Ryan smiled down at Maura. 'Oh, my. Now, you of all people should know I'm worth much more than that. Come on, ladies, what am I worth to you?'

A glance from the corner of his eye showed him the incredulous expression on Molly's face.

Another voice arose. 'Seventy.'

Ryan undid the top buttons of his shirt. 'For my *complete* attention? Don't you think I'm a little more valuable than that?'

Maura raised her chin, a slight smile playing at the corners of her mouth. 'How do we know you're worth any more than that, Ryan?'

Ryan raised an eyebrow and grinned his lop-sided grin. 'Well, if there's any doubt maybe I should just show you.'

'What in hell are you doing?' Molly hissed up at him.

'Marie? Where are you?'

Molly's eyes widened. 'Callaghan!'

Marie Donnelly was pushed through the crowd with 'helping' hands. She smiled up at Ryan, unsure of what was coming.

'Ah, now, there you are.'

In front of the rapt audience he reached down from the stage, offering his hand to the dark-haired woman. 'If you don't mind?'

Molly glanced across at Kate, finding her face as confused as she was sure her own must be. What was he doing? Her eyes moved back to Ryan as Marie placed her hand in his and was helped onto the stage beside him.

As he stood in front of the microphone even his softest words could be heard by the crowd. 'You look very lovely tonight. Would you mind very much if I showed these nice people how valuable I can be?'

There were calls of 'Go on, Marie' and 'Do it, Marie' from the audience. Do *what* exactly? Molly held her breath. He wouldn't!

An expectant silence fell over the room as he stepped towards Marie. The moment he lifted his hand to brush the backs of his fingers along her cheek Molly knew exactly what he was going to do.

'Callaghan, don't you dare!'

Ryan turned his head to look at her. 'Dare what? You want to place a bid, do you, Molly? Because before you do maybe I should just let you know that as of now—' he smiled coolly '—all bets are off.'

She stared at him, this person she suddenly didn't know. She knew what his words were aiming at. The charade was over. Was that all it had been? Not for the Ryan she had known half her life it wouldn't be.

He could only just hear her softly spoken words. 'Why are you doing this?'

'Kissing someone else? There seems to be a lot of that going on tonight, don't you think?'

Her mouth gaped open as he turned his attention back to Marie. The woman glanced apologetically towards her for a moment, before one long finger touched her chin to bring her attention back to Ryan.

'Marie? May I?'

She blinked at him. 'Go on Marie!' To a loud cheer from the assembled crowd, Ryan dipped his head and kissed her.

Molly stared in horror. Watched as he cupped the side of Marie's face, just like he had with her. Watched as he stepped in closer to deepen the kiss.

He had seen it. He had seen Kieran kiss her in the hallway. And now he had put two and two together and got fifty. How could he believe that she would go back to Kieran after all that had happened recently? Didn't he know her well enough to see that she would never have gone into a physical relationship with someone she already cared so much about if she had feelings for someone else?

But here he was, the man she loved, standing on stage in front of a packed room kissing another woman. Molly's heart began to ache in her chest. It hurt. Watching what he was doing really hurt. Never in a million years would she have pulled a stunt like this on him.

'One hundred.'

'One-twenty!'

She glanced across at Kate. Her friend looked stunned. She shrugged her shoulders and raised a questioning eyebrow in Molly's direction. Molly shook her head. Then, with a calmness that surprised herself, she reached her hand into her purse and looked up at the stage, her voice strong.

'Fifty cents.'

Ryan lifted his head and looked down at her. 'What did you say?'

'Fifty cents. It's my bid on you.' She threw the coin at his feet, the noise as it hit the wooden flooring loud in the suddenly silent room. 'It's about all you're worth right now.' And with that she raised her chin, spun on her heel, and walked away from him. A pathway miraculously appeared in the crowd. She even managed to make it outside before the first angry tear appeared.

The house had never felt so empty before. Even when he'd moved in after his return from his crusades to stay in the house that first time without his parents it hadn't been so empty.

Molly was gone.

After a day of sitting in chairs and staring at walls Ryan took himself off to personally chop down as many trees in the park's felling programme as he could before his arms fell off. Or felt like they had. Then he filed and re-filed three years' worth of paperwork in his office. Then he swam four or five miles a day until his legs and arms ached.

But the house stayed empty.

Maybe he should have fought harder. Maybe he should never have thought up that stupid dare in the first place. But then he'd never have held her or kissed her or made love with her. No, he wouldn't trade those memories for anything. Even if he still ached every damn day from wanting her.

After a week he looked like hell. People started noticing. Mrs Collins sent him a casserole. The night guard's wife sent him three tubs of frozen lasagne, which he loathed. Even Mrs Farrelly stopped by the house to see if she could 'help out in any way'.

'Hi, Ryan, how are you?'

He raised empty eyes from his paperwork to look at Kate, where she stood in the open doorway of his office. 'Hey, there.' He forced out a smile. 'Haven't you had that kid yet?'

Kate smiled before sitting down opposite him. She glanced round at the pristine neatness of his office, missing its usual piles of paper. 'No, not yet. Though I feel like I've been carrying this wee one so long it'll just pop on out with a schoolbag and set right off to school.' Her eyes came back to his face. 'Well, you look like hell on legs. So how are you doing?'

Ryan smiled a more genuine smile at her remark. 'Not too good, judging by the number of married women that keep sending me meals to the house.'

Kate pursed her lips. 'Mmm, well, if you ask me you deserve a little suffering.'

'Oh, good. A lecture. Just what I've been missing.'

She ignored him. 'Don't tell me it's not due from someone.'

'I'm sure it is, Kate. But how's about we schedule it for when I'm a little lower? Then you can kick me when I'm *really* down.'

For a moment she almost felt sorry for him. Almost.

'Molly really does love you.'

'Uh-huh.' He leaned back in his chair, linking his hands behind his head. 'I could tell that by how quick she left. Dead giveaway.'

Kate frowned at him. 'As if you gave her a choice! You really are a bloody idiot, aren't you? If I'd known that when I was sixteen I'd have mooned round after you a lot less.'

Ryan's eyes widened. 'You never mooned after me, Kate.'

'You see, now, that's exactly how much you noticed. You were too busy following round after some redhead we both know.'

'I'm sorry.' He looked repentant.

'Mmm.' Kate softened a little. 'Well, it's okay. I got over you.'

A smile. 'I'm glad.'

'Pity I won't be able to say the same for Molly.'

He sighed. 'Oh, Molly will get over me. In fact I'd say she's pretty much over being over me by now.'

Kate leaned forward as best she could to wag her forefinger at him. 'Don't you dare lay the blame on her doorstep. This is *your* fault.'

He unlinked his hands, bouncing his chair forward. 'Probably.'

'Definitely.'

'Well, now that's settled.' He stood up. 'I believe I have trees to chop down. So if you'll excuse me.'

'I want to know what you're going to do.'

Ryan reached out for his waterproof jacket, then threw it down on his desk in frustration. 'What do you want me to do, Kate? Suffer a bit more? 'Cos let me tell you I don't think that's possible.'

'You could go get her back.'

'Well, how stupid of me! Of course that's what I could do.' He snapped his fingers in front of his face. 'I'll just drive down to Dublin, beat Kieran to a pulp—which, incidentally, I *really* want to do—and then throw her over my shoulder and carry her back here. Now, where did I leave those car keys?' He looked around the office.

Kate ignored him until he looked at her again. 'You finished?'

He dropped down onto the edge of his desk, his shoulders slumped despondently. A wry smile appeared. 'Days ago, if that matters.' Then he shook his head. 'Look, if it makes this any better for you, I know how much I've lost, okay? And it hurts like hell. Satisfied?'

Again she studied him. 'No.'

Ryan exploded. 'Well, what the hell else do you want from me?'

'I want you to admit you're in love with her.'

'God! Is that all? Fine.' He ran his fingers through his already unruly hair. 'I'm so in love with Molly that I can't breathe properly when she's not around. I never bloody well have, okay?'

Kate smiled gently, her voice soothing. 'Then try telling her, Ryan. She could do with hearing it.'

'I can't.'

She was completely knocked back by the raw pain on his face. It was as if someone had just removed a limb from his body without an anaesthetic. 'Why ever not?'

'I've been trying to for nearly twelve years and I've never even got close. I only just survived when I lost my mother and father, Kate. I survived *because* there was Molly. If I ever completely lost her then I'm not sure I could keep going. At least if she's happy with Kieran I can still take a shot at trying to be her friend again. Given time.'

He held his arms out in surrender. 'So what on earth makes you think I can tell her now? I lost my chance the day she met him.'

Molly had never felt so empty in her entire life. Before, when she'd been lonely, there'd been Ryan. Before, when she'd felt lost, there'd been Ryan. Scared—there was Ryan. Confused? He was still there for her. Now she had her worst nightmare. No Ryan, in any shape or form.

It felt like hell.

He hadn't come home the night of the auction so she'd been able to pack on her own. So little to show for her stay in his house. She hadn't even realised until she'd packed it all away.

Her first day without him had been spent alternately hating his guts and sobbing her heart out. Then she'd tidied her half-finished house from top to bottom. After that, she'd cried some more. She swam a few miles every evening when the water was cold.

A week later she knew she probably looked like hell and had no tears left. That stupid, dumb bet. Maybe she should have just left and gone back to the States. But a new photographic contract for wildlife shots in the park had come in. And Kate was due to give birth any day, so Molly would be needed at the shop....

All good excuses, she knew. But she realised the truth was that she *couldn't* leave again. Not now. Regardless of whether she could ever look at Ryan again, she was finally home. Home is where the heart is. And Molly's heart and soul were in the small corner of the world where Ryan was. That was the simple fact.

Kate came to see her. She waddled around Molly's house, studying each room intently and never once mentioning Ryan.

Molly made tea and joined her on the decking at the rear of the house. 'So, how's the store?'

'Oh, it's just grand. That new kid is doing all right, y'know.'

Molly nodded. 'That's good, then.'

'Mmm.' Kate glanced back at the house. 'This place will be nice when it's finished. I always did like the lough from the Doon side.'

'Me too. That's why I bought this place soon as I saw

it. There's even a pathway to the shore through those trees.' She jerked her head in the direction of the pathway. 'I've got some great shots of the geese at first light, with the mist still on the water.'

Kate nodded. 'That's nice.'

Molly sipped at her tea. 'So. How are you and the baby?'

Kate patted her stomach. 'We're only about twenty months overdue now.'

'Oh, well, that's all right, then.'

More tea sipping. Then Molly raised an eyebrow. 'And how is Paul holding up?'

Kate exploded. 'Oh, for crying out loud, Molly. Why don't you ask me how Ryan is? It's not like you're busting to know or anything!'

Molly blinked with wide, sad eyes. 'Okay, fine—how is he?'

'Oh, he's just grand, if you think the zombie look is attractive.'

Molly stood up and walked towards the edge of the decking. She'd thought she was finished with the crying thing. Apparently not. And to think she'd always avoided overly emotional females.

'Yes, he looks as bad as you do at the minute. If you ask me the two of you need your heads banging together. Why on earth you would prefer being this miserable to being together stuns me.'

'It's not out of choice.'

'Isn't it?'

'Oh, right. I get it.' She spun on her friend with glistening eyes. 'This is all *my* fault 'cos I chose to leave, right? That's what you're getting at. Nothing at all to do with the fact that he kissed another woman in front of the entire town to get back at me for something I hadn't even done.'

'I didn't say that.'

'No, but it's what you thought.'

'But the two of you were so happy! You walked around grinning like idiots the whole time.' Kate shook her head. 'So what went wrong?'

Molly seemed to deflate before Kate's eyes, all the fight draining out of her. She looked towards the lough. 'He gave up on me. If he'd loved me even half as much as I love him then he would never have given up. And I can't settle for half, Kate. I want it all—' Her voice broke. 'I wanted my best friend to fall head over heels in love with me.'

'He did.'

She brushed a hand across her face. 'No, he didn't.' A loud sniff. 'No. You see, Ryan fights for the things he loves the most. Hell, he fought for stupid rainforests more than he fought to keep me. How could he even for one second think I'd go back to that—that rat's ass?'

'Rainforests aren't stupid.'

'I know.' Another loud sniff.

Kate looked at her friend's sad face. This was just awful. 'Maybe he's scared, Molly.'

'Ryan Callaghan, superhero? I don't think so.'

'It's possible.'

'Well, in that case he was obviously less scared of losing me than he was of taking a chance on us. That's real reassuring!'

'Maybe he was scared of the same things you would be if you were in his shoes.'

'Like what?'

Kate sighed dramatically. 'Oh, you know—the usual stuff. Maybe you didn't love him as much as he wanted you to. Maybe you really belonged with Kieran. Maybe you'd run off to the States and break his heart again—'

'I never broke his heart by going to the States!'

Blue eyes stared directly into green. 'Didn't you?'

Molly stared back. 'Kate, did I? Did I break his heart when I left?'

'Which time?'

The first time he saw her she was dancing with Nick Scallon. It had been two weeks of hell and chopping trees. And the first time he braved a social gathering there she was. With bloody Nick Scallon!

He marched straight up to them on the hotel dance floor, all eyes in the room burning holes into his back. 'What in God's name are you doing here?'

Molly raised an eyebrow, then glared at him. 'I believe it's called dancing.'

Ryan stared at her in complete amazement.

'Go away, Callaghan.'

'Like hell I will.'

'Look, Ryan.' Nick turned to look at him. 'I believe the lady said for you to leave. I don't think she wants to talk to you.'

Ryan glared at him dangerously. 'Unless you plan on eating your own teeth for dinner, I suggest you stay out of this.'

'Ryan!'

'I mean it—he better stay out of it.'

'Stay out of what, exactly?'

For a moment he looked dumbfounded. 'Well…'

Molly raised both eyebrows. 'Well?'

His eyes scanned the room, ignoring the fact they'd become the floorshow for the evening yet again. 'Where is Kieran?'

'Who?'

'Oh, you know rightly who.'

She appeared to think for a moment, then clicked her fingers. 'Oh, you mean *Kieran*—the guy you *gave* me to.

Well, now, my guess would be that he's in Dublin some-where—with his fiancée.'

Cold eyes looked him up and down before turning to shine on Nick. 'Now, Nick, if you don't mind I think we'll go somewhere else. I don't much care for the crowd in here.'

'Wait.' One large hand grasped her arm. 'You didn't go back with Kieran?'

Nick stepped between them, removing Ryan's hand. 'Why don't you just leave her alone, Ryan? I think she's made it perfectly clear she doesn't want to speak to you.'

With a wry smile Ryan glanced at Nick from the corner of his eye. 'I did warn you.' And with that Ryan punched him. Hard enough to put him on the floor.

'For crying out loud!' Molly yelled. 'What are you do-ing?'

She dropped down beside Nick. 'Nick, are you all right?'

'I warned him.' Ryan justified his action while nursing his bruised fist. 'Where have you been if you haven't been with Kieran?'

'Go to hell!'

Ryan laughed. 'Been there, done that.'

Molly stood up, helping Nick to his feet before standing off against Ryan. 'You are a complete moron—you know that? Who the hell do you think you are? When you *gave* me to Kieran you gave up all prior claims. So you can just butt out of my life—you hear?'

'You kissed him!'

'You kissed Marie Donnelly!'

'That was different!'

'The hell it was!'

Ryan blinked, then frowned. 'Fine. Fine, have it your way.'

'Fine.'

'Good.'

'Yeah, right.' Ryan stormed off the dance floor, nursing his hand.

Molly marched right after him. She couldn't help herself. 'Oh, and by the way, tough guy, that friend you were so eager to give me to?'

Ryan swung round, his face dark. 'What about him?'

'He screwed around.'

'What?'

At the look of complete shock on his face Molly almost softened. But it was about time he had the facts. 'Yep, just shortly after I figured out he wasn't the guy for me, he went and proved I was right. Several times. So what makes you think I would want to stick around for more?'

A variety of emotions crossed his expressive face. Then he shook his head, his eyes sad. 'I had no idea. I'm so sorry. If I'd known…'

Green eyes stared up into chocolate-brown. 'Yeah, well, that's why I didn't tell you. I knew exactly what you'd do.' She glanced around the room, her voice lowering. 'But, like I've told you before, Callaghan, I'm crap at relationships. *You've* proved that, haven't you?'

She turned away, walking back towards her table and Nick.

'Molly?'

Her softly spoken name halted her steps. But she just couldn't look at him again. If she did she wouldn't be able to walk away. And she knew it. 'What?'

'Why did you kiss him?'

'I didn't.' She sighed, '*He* kissed *me*. If you'd waited ten seconds you'd have seen exactly what I thought of him doing that.'

The music changed in the background, and a soulful

country and western song filled the silence. Molly held her breath.

'I've really screwed this up, haven't I?'

She looked at her feet, her eyes blinking rapidly as she tried to stay in control. 'It was that stupid bet, Ryan. *It* screwed things up. Maybe we'd have been better if we'd just stayed the way we were.'

Ryan stared at her back for a long moment. 'What do I have to do to make this right again?'

'If you don't know by now, Callaghan, then I can't tell you.' Her eyes blinked harder as she looked towards the ceiling.

She waited for a few moments, but when Ryan said nothing she walked away, even managing to get to Nick before glancing over her shoulder. But he was gone.

'That's quite a right hook your boyfriend has.' Nick smiled wryly as she joined him. 'Must be all that outdoors work he does.'

Molly was suitably embarrassed. 'I'm so sorry, Nick. I had no idea he would hit you.'

Nick smiled at his date. 'You did warn me he might be upset if he saw us.'

'Mmm.' She looked towards the doorway. 'But, still, it's not like Ryan to just run round hitting people all over the place.'

'The man's tortured. I have to say he looks like hell.'

Molly had noticed too. For a moment she'd wanted to reach out for him, to comfort him. But if he was stupid enough not to see how she felt then why should she help him out of his torment?

Nick's blue eyes studied her profile for a few silent moments. 'It must be something to love someone as much as you love each other.'

Molly turned sad green eyes towards him. 'Oh, yeah, it's

something, all right.' She reached a hand towards his cheek, turning his swollen eye towards her. 'I really am sorry. If I'd thought this would happen I would never have involved you.'

He placed his hand over hers, turning her palm to his lips to place a kiss there. 'It's entirely my pleasure, Molly. I've been wanting a date with you since I first saw you, and at least this way I can say I went out with you before you settled down.'

'You know, Nick Scallon, you're not that bad after all.'

He smiled. 'Why don't you put him out of his misery, Molly?'

'Why don't I go tell him how much I love him and all that?'

He nodded. 'Yeah, all that.'

She glanced towards the doorway, then back into Nick's eyes. 'Honestly?'

With a gentle squeeze of her fingers, he released her hand. 'Honestly.'

'I'm scared to death he won't feel the same way I do.'

Nick smiled broadly. 'Honey, I really don't think you've got a problem there.'

Molly smiled weakly. 'I guess a part of me knows that, but I just need him to tell me it too. I'm only human; I need the words.'

'I'm pretty sure they're there. I'd say your friend is just struggling with a way to say them.'

'God, I hope you're right.'

'You *knew*.'

Kate glanced up at his angry face. 'Knew what, exactly?'

'You knew she didn't leave with Kieran.'

Her face stayed calm. 'Everybody knew.'

'I didn't know!' he yelled down at her.

'Well.' A shrug. 'There you go, then.'

'So where has she been all this time?'

Kate frustrated him further by leaving to serve some customers. The moment they left he rounded on her. 'So?'

'So what?' Again she blinked.

Ryan looked as if he'd explode at any second and leave goo all over the walls. His face was red with rage. 'Kate, I want to know where she's been since she left my house.'

Kate placed her hands on her hips and glared up at him. 'Do you make a habit of bullying pregnant women?'

'Kate!'

'Okay, okay.' She held her hands up in surrender. 'It's not like it's some big secret. Everyone knew she had moved into her house.'

Ryan practically pouted. '*I* didn't know.'

'You didn't ask.'

Her words silenced him momentarily. 'Why would I have asked unless I'd known she hadn't left?'

'You just assumed she had.' Kate returned to her seat. 'Just like you assumed she'd want to go back to Kieran in the first place.'

'Yes, well, I have information now that I didn't have then.'

'She told you about the other women?'

Ryan looked as if he'd like to punch something. 'She should have told me then.'

'So you could beat him to a pulp? Maybe she thought it would be better to keep you out of prison.' Kate hid a smile.

'I don't even think I like the guy very much.'

'Yeah, you and half the population. Poor Neave.'

'I'm sure she'll find out eventually.'

'Oh, I think she had a fairly good idea before they left.'

Ryan stared. 'You didn't?'

'Who, me? As if I would do such a thing!' She blinked innocently. 'But I may have suggested that Kieran wanted to speak to her in the hallway about something just before the auction started....'

Ryan laughed for the first time in days. 'You're incredible! Remind me to remember that the next time I'm making such a mess of things, will you?'

Kate raised an eyebrow at him. 'Mmm. You owe Marie Donnelly an apology as well, you know. Just while I'm sorting out the world, I thought I'd remind you.'

He had the good grace to blush. 'Yeah, I know. She gave me a real ear-bashing after Molly left. I sent her flowers and an apology note.'

'That's another reason you need Molly in your life. She's the only one who ever sticks up for you. Otherwise the women in this town would have to slap you around the head a couple of times a day to keep you in line.'

'I'm an idiot, aren't I?'

A smile broke free. 'Now, are you asking me or telling me?'

Ryan slapped the front of his head with the palm of his hand. Suddenly things were all too clear to him. 'Oh, my God, what an idiot!'

''Bout time. So now what are you going to do?'

'It's backfired on you, Molly.'

She stared at Kate. 'What do you mean?'

'The whole Nick Scallon ''in your face, Ryan'' scam that you tried.'

Molly shrugged her shoulders and looked away. 'I haven't the faintest idea what you mean.'

'Yeah, I'll bet you don't. Well, whatever it was, it backfired. So you've no one to blame but yourself. If you'd just swallowed your pride, spoken to him, told him how you felt, then you could both be grinning your heads off now.'

Without looking up from her bookwork Molly continued playing innocent. 'Backfired how?'

'He quit.'

That got her attention. 'What the hell do you mean, he quit?'

'Ryan.' Kate frowned. 'He quit his job. A month's notice, I hear.'

Molly stared at her in shock.

Kate stared right back. 'Well?'

'Where is he going?'

'And why would you care?'

'Kate!'

'I wish people would stop saying my name in that tone of voice. It's really annoying.'

'Oh, for goodness' sake, Kate, will you just tell me where he's going?'

'No. I'm serious—why would you care? You want to torture him a little longer? See what other men you can dangle under his nose before he kills one of them?'

Molly stared at her friend in shock, her voice shaky. 'How can you think that? You know how I feel—you of all people.'

Kate looked away for a moment. 'Well, it wasn't nice what you did. There's been entirely too much of that stuff going on. And I told Ryan as much too. You know Marie gave him a hard time about kissing her in front of you?'

'She did? That was nice of her.' Molly looked down at the counter, guilt washing across her conscience at all the nasty thoughts she'd had about the woman. She sighed. 'I thought Ryan might at the very least be jealous enough to realise what he was losing if I went out with Nick. But I didn't tell Nick any lies, Kate. He knew how I felt—how

I *feel* about Ryan. When he visited me at the house his invitation was a neighbourly one. Nothing more.'

There was strained silence as Molly struggled to hold another bout of tears at bay. 'How can he just leave, Kate? He loves this place; it's his life.'

Kate smiled softly at her friend's bowed head. 'He loves *you*. He's not about to stand around watching you go out with someone else.'

Molly's head snapped upwards. 'Then why in hell won't he say so? Is it going to cost him so much?' Her eyes sparked with anger and unshed tears. 'Where on earth does the ridiculous lump think he's going to go, anyway?'

'Someone mentioned something about endangered tigers, or something, somewhere...' She watched as Molly ran out of the shop. 'Hey, where are you going? Molly?' Then she smiled. 'Ha.'

Ryan wasn't in his office. Running frantically from the foyer, Molly scanned the harbour with desperate eyes. Then she saw him, his tall frame standing on the far jetty. He was talking to a long line of tourists as they waited for the lough's tour boat.

Ryan had spent most of the morning waiting for her arrival. He first saw her when she reached the middle of the jetty, his face immediately softening into an affectionate smile. 'Hey, O'Brien.'

'Don't you "Hey, O'Brien" me, you great blundering idiot!'

He blinked at her, then pointed at his chest. 'Who? Me?'

'Yes, you.' She turned and smiled sweetly at the line of tourists. 'Hi, how are you folks today? Nice holiday so far?'

There was a mumbled chorus of 'great' and 'real good' while she turned back on Ryan. 'So you quit, did you?

Twice in one month? That must be a record even by your standards.'

'Now, O'Brien...'

She smiled sweetly over his shoulder at the tourists. 'It's a lovely part of Ireland here, isn't it?'

The smile vanished as she looked back at him. 'You couldn't just stay and fight to keep me, could you, Callaghan?'

'If you'd just listen—'

'What part of the world are you from yourself?' she asked an American, and didn't wait for an answer. 'I mean, you fight so damned hard for everything else, so why couldn't you put up the smallest whimper of a struggle to keep me?'

'I thought—'

'Oh, no you didn't, Ryan. Thinking never once entered into it.'

'If you'd just wait a minute—'

'Are you guys staying for long, then?' She smiled at the crowd again.

'Molly, please—'

She glared at him, her eyes glittering. 'Please what? Calm down? Don't talk about it here? What is it? Am I scaring you? Well, you know what? I hope I am.'

Ryan reached out towards her. 'We can talk about this and sort it out; I know we can. I just had to get you here so I could do this face to face. If you'll just let me tell you—'

'And hasn't the weather been great for you?' she demanded of the American, interrupting Ryan's speech. 'You were just going to find another crusade, I take it? Get yourself killed somewhere rather than trying to stay here?'

'Molly—'

'Why travel all that distance when I can help you out

right here? After all, you could drown as handy as get savaged by dumb tigers!'

Without any warning she shoved him square in the chest with all her strength. It had the desired effect. The move was so sudden it caught Ryan off balance. He lost his footing, falling off the jetty and into the lough. The enormous splash was equivalent to his size.

'I really hope you enjoy the rest of your visit.' She smiled sweetly at the line of shocked faces. Then, spinning on her heel, head held high, she marched back down the jetty and across the harbour.

'Molly!' Ryan spluttered as he yelled across at her. 'Molly, for crying out loud, will you wait for just a minute?'

Several of the tourists photographed him as he dragged himself onto the jetty. He managed to smile lop-sidedly at them. 'Red-haired women. You gotta watch out for them.'

'And that ain't no lie!' An American grinned at his red-headed wife. 'Ain't that true, honey?'

'You wanna go swimmin' too, sweetie?'

'No, ma'am.'

'Molly!' He ran after her, his boots squelching with every step. 'Will you just stop?'

She kept on marching. Her foot was about to step onto the stone stairs off the harbour when he yelled across at her, 'O'Brien, I didn't quit my job. I'm not going anywhere.'

Molly stopped. Ryan stopped running and waited. The wheels in her head turned slowly. He wasn't leaving. But Kate had said… Kate. She looked up at the foyer and Kate waved at her with a grin. Shaking her head, Molly resumed walking.

'Did you hear me?' His voice sounded desperate. 'It was the only way I knew for sure I could get you to come and see me.' He shook his head. 'Aw, c'mon, O'Brien. Are you gonna make me do this here?'

She lifted her chin as she walked, almost clear of the harbour before he spoke again. This time his voice was louder. 'Molly O'Brien, would you please put us both out of this damn misery and just marry me?'

Molly froze. Taking a deep breath, she slowly turned to face him. 'Now, why on God's earth would I want to do something as stupid as that?'

Ryan shrugged and held out his hands, his sweater sleeves stretching like wings with the weight of water. 'Because I'm so in love with you that that I can't think straight when you're not around?'

She folded her arms across her chest to stop her heart from beating its way out through it. 'Oh, I *see*. And when exactly did you reach this astonishing revelation?'

'Oh, I guess—give or take a month or two—about twelve years ago.'

She faltered. Ryan started to walk towards her while tourists grinned ridiculously at him. A crowd started to form as the tour boat pulled in.

'It was on your birthday.'

Her eyes widened. 'My eighteenth?'

'You told me you were in love with Kieran, and even though I knew that I couldn't take my eyes off you.'

'You couldn't?'

Passengers off-loaded from the boat, but the new passengers refused to get aboard. The boat's skipper got onto the jetty. 'What's happening?'

'It was really rotten feeling, being so disloyal to Kieran, but I couldn't help it. After all, I saw you first.'

Molly smiled slightly. 'You did, didn't you?'

Ryan kept walking towards her, his steps slower now,

his voice lower. 'You held me together when my family died.'

Her breath caught.

He continued, 'I thought I'd never get over it, but you stayed with me and I didn't want anyone else there but you. Just you. I didn't want to let you go.'

'I just wanted to take it all away from you, Callaghan. I loved you so much, and when you were hurting I hurt too. It was just always like that. For you too.'

Ryan stopped for a moment. 'I know.'

'Honey, are you getting on the boat?'

The woman waved a hand at her husband. 'You just shush. I'm not goin' anywheres 'til I see these nice folks kiss and make up.'

'Twelve years, Ryan? All that time and you never said a word?'

Another shrug, and again he moved closer. 'You left me.' He smiled warmly. 'Twice, if I remember correctly. I even came to fetch you once. And I kept on asking you to come home, didn't I?'

Molly nodded. 'Maybe if you'd told me the reason I'd have come home sooner.'

He stopped in front of her, the air held still in his chest. Then his dark eyes looked down into the green depth of hers. 'What finally brought you home O'Brien?'

At last she smiled. 'You. I came home to you, Callaghan. I thought you always knew I would.'

'Why?' The word was a whisper as he made love to her with his eyes.

'Because I'm in love with you. I've loved you ever since I met you. It just took me a while to admit what it was. It's such a big, scary thing, Ryan. It's what everything else in my life moves around. Loving you.'

A smile. 'I know.'

'So why did you give up, dumbass?'

'You really thought, after all that's happened between us, that I could go back to Kieran?'

'I thought I lost you to him a long time ago.' He reached out to touch the side of her face, his eyes stormy. 'I'm sorry, Molly. Sorry that I couldn't see what was right in front of my face. The one thing in my life I should have fought the hardest for was one thing I was most afraid to lose.'

Her smaller hand covered his against her face. 'You wouldn't have lost me, you idiot. I might have let us both suffer a little longer, but eventually I'd have come back to kick your butt and ask you why you hadn't come to get me. You know me. I never could leave well enough alone—not when it concerned you.'

He smiled into her eyes. 'I've waited a long time for you. Come home with me—to *our* home—to stay?'

Molly nodded, her gaze steady. 'Uh-huh.'

Ryan smiled his lop-sided grin at her for several happy moments. 'Hey, O'Brien?'

Molly tilted her chin towards him. 'What, Callaghan?'

'I have a little wager for you.'

She laughed. 'Oh, really? And what might that be, then? 'Cos I should warn you, I've sworn off those things.'

'Okay, then—a dare. I dare you to spend the rest of your life with me.'

She glanced around at their audience, and then smiled back at him. 'I'll take that dare.'

They stood for a long moment smiling at each other, then he leaned forward. 'About those twelve kids...'

Her green eyes widened.

'Oh, and by the way, watch out—dip ahead.'

As flashes went off and cameras clicked Ryan dipped

her back in his arms and kissed her. A ripple of applause echoed across the harbour.

Back in the foyer, Kate grinned widely. 'It's about time, too.' Then she grasped her stomach and looked down. 'Oh, well, *your* timing is just great, isn't it?'

Curl up and have a

Heart *to* Heart

with

Harlequin Romance®

Just like having a heart-to-heart
with your best friend, these stories
will take you from laughter to tears
and back again. So heartwarming
and emotional you'll want to
have some tissues handy!

Introducing the third book in this new,
emotionally gratifying miniseries

A Family for Keeps
by Lucy Gordon
On sale May 2005

Available wherever Harlequin books are sold.

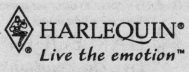

If you enjoyed what you just read,
then we've got an offer you can't resist!

Take 2 bestselling love stories FREE!
Plus get a FREE surprise gift!

Clip this page and mail it to Harlequin Reader Service®

IN U.S.A.	IN CANADA
3010 Walden Ave.	P.O. Box 609
P.O. Box 1867	Fort Erie, Ontario
Buffalo, N.Y. 14240-1867	L2A 5X3

YES! Please send me 2 free Harlequin Romance® novels and my free surprise gift. After receiving them, if I don't wish to receive anymore, I can return the shipping statement marked cancel. If I don't cancel, I will receive 6 brand-new novels every month, before they're available in stores! In the U.S.A., bill me at the bargain price of $3.57 plus 25¢ shipping & handling per book and applicable sales tax, if any*. In Canada, bill me at the bargain price of $4.05 plus 25¢ shipping & handling per book and applicable taxes**. That's the complete price and a savings of 10% off the cover prices—what a great deal! I understand that accepting the 2 free books and gift places me under no obligation ever to buy any books. I can always return a shipment and cancel at any time. Even if I never buy another book from Harlequin, the 2 free books and gift are mine to keep forever.

186 HDN DZ72
386 HDN DZ73

Name		(PLEASE PRINT)	
Address			Apt.#
City		State/Prov.	Zip/Postal Code

Not valid to current Harlequin Romance® subscribers.
Want to try another series? Call 1-800-873-8635
or visit www.morefreebooks.com.

* Terms and prices subject to change without notice. Sales tax applicable in N.Y.
** Canadian residents will be charged applicable provincial taxes and GST.
   All orders subject to approval. Offer limited to one per household.
   ® are registered trademarks owned and used by the trademark owner and or its licensee.

HROM04R   ©2004 Harlequin Enterprises Limited

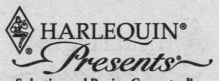

HARLEQUIN®
Presents

Seduction and Passion Guaranteed!

Legally wed, but he's never said…
"I love you."

They're…

Wedlocked!

The series
in which
marriages are
made in haste…
and love
comes later…

**Look out for more Wedlocked! marriage stories
in Harlequin Presents throughout 2005.**

Coming in May:
THE DISOBEDIENT BRIDE
by Helen Bianchin
#2463

Coming in June:
THE MORETTI MARRIAGE
by Catherine Spencer
#2474

HARLEQUIN®
Presents·

Seduction and Passion Guaranteed!

Introducing a brand-new trilogy by

Sharon Kendrick

THE
ROYAL HOUSE
OF
CACCIATORE

*Passion, power & privilege – the dynasty continues
with these handsome princes...*

Welcome to Mardivino—a beautiful and wealthy
Mediterranean island principality, with a prestigious
and glamorous royal family. There are three
Cacciatore princes—Nicolo, Guido and
the eldest, the heir, Gianferro.

Next month (May 05), meet Nico in
THE MEDITERRANEAN
PRINCE'S PASSION #2466

Coming in June: Guido's story, in
THE PRINCE'S LOVE-CHILD #2472

Coming soon: Gianferro's story in
THE FUTURE KING'S BRIDE

Only from Harlequin Presents

www.eHarlequin.com   HPRHC